THE JUDGEMENT O

The Judgemen

First published in eBook and paperback
2024

© Wyatt Steele

The right of Wyatt Steele to be identified as the author of this work has been asserted by her in accordance with the Copyright, Designs and Patents Act 1988.

All rights reserved. No part of this publication may be reproduced, stored in or introduced into a retrieval system, or transmitted, in any form, or by any means (electronic, mechanical, photocopying, recording or otherwise) without the prior written permission of the writer. Any person who does any unauthorized act in rclation to this publication may be liable to criminal prosecution and civil claims for damages.

Thank you for respecting the hard work of this author.

Contents

PREFACE 6

INTRODUCTION 8

CHAPTER ONE 16

CHAPTER TWO 26

CHAPTER THREE 34

CHAPTER FOUR 41

CHAPTER FIVE 56

CHAPTER SIX 65

CHAPTER SEVEN 77

CHAPTER EIGHT 88

CHAPTER NINE 98

CHAPTER TEN 112

CHAPTER ELEVEN 131

CHAPTER TWELVE 144

CHAPTER THIRTEEN 155

CHAPTER FOURTEEN 166

CHAPTER FIFTEEN 179

PREFACE

Wyatt Steele's great grand pappy came from Dublin. A writer by trade, Declan Kelly had worked on the Irish Times and the so-called Freeman's Journal, reporting on politics and social injustice. In the late 1880's he crossed the Atlantic, arriving in New York he secured work with the Herald Newspaper. The newspaper regularly carried sensational stories, and so Declan headed out West to find some new material for the Herald.

During his travels Declan met many people, and he recorded their lives in his diaries. These are not tales of the old West; these are the firsthand reports from those involved of what happened. Most of the details in the diaries never made it into print. The diaries were passed to my father's father, then to my father and then about ten years ago to me. I'd heard some of the tales they included recounted to me by my father and grandfather in years gone past, but reading them again, and finding new stories of the lives of those long since gone, of the hardship they endured made me want to share these with those interested in this time period. This is the first, and hopefully not the last, of the stories from my grand pappy's diaries. The people you will read about in the following pages existed, the struggles they endured very real, this is not a work of fiction but a recount of an incident in their lives that shaped them.

This book is written in the style of the classic western, but remember, as you turn the pages that the events happened, they are based on the recollections of those who survived. The hopes, dreams, pain and fear were once felt by these people in a very real sense. Their experiences were written down when the events were fresh in their minds and their nerves still raw from what had just happened.

INTRODUCTION

The Ironwood Savings Bank was a fortress in name only. Its brick façade and iron-banded doors gave an illusion of security, but inside, men who feared for their lives held the keys. Still, it had been enough to lull the townsfolk into a false sense of safety—a mistake the gang planned to exploit.

The air inside was thick with dust and fear. The heavy afternoon heat pressed against the windows, amplifying the muffled sobs of a young teller sprawled on the floor behind the counter. Four other townsfolk huddled nearby, their faces pale and eyes wide with terror. The lead outlaw, a man with a jagged scar deep above his left eyebrow, stood in the center of the bank, his revolver held steady, the barrel gleaming faintly in the sunlight streaming through the dirty windows. His eyes above the bandana that covered his face were as hard as flint.

"Clock's ticking," the scarred man growled, his voice low and gravelly, eyes darting to the bank manager, a balding man whose hands trembled as he fumbled with a keyring.

"I—I'm trying!" the manager stammered, sweat beading on his forehead. He knelt before the vault, the massive steel door looming over him like a judgment. Each shake of his hands made the keys jingle, the sound almost absurdly loud in the tense silence.

"Try harder," barked another outlaw, younger, leaner, and with a nervous energy that made his trigger finger twitch. His rifle was aimed lazily at the hostages, but his eyes flicked to the door every few seconds. "We ain't got all day."

Outside, the sound of hoofbeats could be heard echoing faintly in the street as wagons passed. The town of Ironwood was carrying on business, completely unaware of the nightmare unfolding behind the bank's façade.

The scarred man's patience snapped. He strode forward, grabbed the manager by the collar, and yanked him to his feet. "You think we're playin', old man? Open that vault now, or I'll start pickin' hostages to decorate the walls!"

The manager whimpered, his shaking hands finally finding the right key. With a metallic clunk, the lock gave way, and the vault door creaked open. The outlaws surged forward, their boots scuffing against the worn wooden floor.

Stacks of bills and gold bars gleamed in the dim light of the vault. The younger outlaw let out a long, low whistle, causing the bandana across his face to flutter. "Ain't that a sight?"

"Bag it up," the scarred man ordered, tossing burlap sacks toward his men. They moved quickly, loading the loot with practiced efficiency. Outside, the faint murmur of townsfolk drifted through the walls, a reminder of how precariously their plan hung in the balance.

The sound of jangling spurs shattered the moment. All heads snapped toward the door as a shadow fell across the frosted glass. Someone was approaching. The scarred man raised a hand, signaling silence. The younger outlaw froze, his finger hovering over the trigger of his rifle.

The door swung open with a creak, letting in a gust of hot, dry air and the heavy scent of dust and horse sweat. A portly man in a wide-brimmed hat stepped inside, tugging at the collar of his sweat-stained shirt, his face flushed from the relentless heat. His boot heels clunked against the wooden floor, and he froze mid-step, his eyes widening as they swept over the tense scene—hostages huddled in the corner, the telltale glint of steel in the hands of men with murder in their eyes.

"Well, now," the scarred man drawled, his voice dripping with amusement as he turned to face the newcomer. His lips curled into a slow, predatory grin, eyes dark with the thrill of control. "Look what the cat dragged in."

The man swallowed hard, his Adam's apple bobbing as he raised his hands in a placating gesture, lips parting to plead—or maybe just to breathe through the sudden weight of fear pressing down on him.

He never got the chance.

The scarred outlaw's revolver barked, the explosion of sound echoing through the bank like a thunderclap. The bullet struck the man square in the chest, lifting him clean off his feet. His body jerked backward as if yanked by an invisible hand, his hat flying off and spinning through the air like a dying bird. The force of the shot propelled him through the swinging bank doors, which crashed open with a violent slap against the outer walls.

For a split second, time seemed to pause—dust motes dancing in the streaks of sunlight that filtered through the open doors, the stunned silence that hung in the air thick enough to choke on. Then came the sickening thud as his body hit the wooden planks outside, sprawling in a lifeless heap, blood already pooling beneath him and seeping into the cracks of the weathered boards.

The teller whimpered a thin, high-pitched sound that made the scarred man's grin widen. He twirled his gun once, sliding it back into his holster with a casual ease that suggested he'd done this sort of thing too many times to count.

"Guess he wasn't withdrawin' nothin' today," he said with a chuckle, his gaze sweeping over the remaining hostages like a wolf eyeing trapped prey. "Anyone else got a hankerin' to play hero?"

No one moved. No one breathed.

The outlaws exchanged glances, the weight of the moment thickening around them like the gathering storm outside. The only sound was the distant, fading echo of gunfire and the eerie creak of the bank doors swinging in the afternoon breeze.

"Anyone else got questions?" the scarred man growled, his voice cold. He turned back to his men. "Wrap it up! We're leavin'."

The outlaws hefted the sack and bolted for the back door, the scarred man bringing up the rear. They burst into the alley, where their horses were tied and ready.

"Move!" the scarred man barked, vaulting into his saddle. The others followed suit.

As the gang thundered out of Ironwood, their horses kicking up plumes of dust, the scarred man allowed himself a grim smile. They'd pulled it off.

But as the distant cries of alarm bells began to echo behind them, he couldn't shake the feeling that the trouble had only just begun.

The gang's horses pounded the dirt, their hooves kicking up a blinding cloud as they tore through the outskirts of Ironwood. The scarred man rode at the front, his grim smile hidden beneath the shadow of his hat. They'd done it—fast, clean, and bloody enough to make the townsfolk think twice before chasing after them.

Then, just as they veered onto the main trail leading out of town, a lone figure leading a tired donkey stepped into their path. His eyes were on the ground before him, and he couldn't see them straight away.

It was an older man dressed in a faded shirt, his face weathered by years under the sun. His wide-brimmed hat sat slightly askew, and in one hand, he clutched the reins of a mule loaded with sacks of grain. His eyes widened as he took in the sight of the armed riders bearing down on him.

"Hold it there!" the scarred man barked, pulling his horse to a skidding stop. The rest of the gang followed suit, dust swirling around them as they drew their guns. The old man froze, his mouth working silently as he raised one hand in a shaky gesture of surrender.

"Please," the man croaked, his voice dry with fear. "I don't want no trouble."

The scarred man tilted his head, studying the figure before him. "Trouble's already here, old-timer," he said, his voice low and edged with menace. "What're you doin' out here?"

The old man licked his lips, his free hand gripping the mule's bridle tightly. "Just bringin' supplies back to my farm," he said quickly. "Didn't see nothin', swear it."

The scarred man's lips twitched into a faint, humorless smile. "Didn't see nothin', huh?"

The old man nodded frantically, his voice trembling and his hands wrong the rope he held. "That's right. Just passin' through, is all."

For a moment, it seemed like the gang might let him go. But then the scarred man's smile vanished, replaced by a cold, calculating look. "Can't have you remembering faces," he said flatly.

The old man's eyes widened in understanding, and he took a step back. "Wait—" he began, but the scarred man had already drawn his revolver.

The crack of the gunshot echoed through the empty street, sharp and final. The old man crumpled to the ground, the mule braying in panic and bolting into the brush. The scarred man holstered his weapon without so much as a glance at the body.

"Let's move," the scarred man barked, his voice sharp with authority. "We've wasted enough time."

As they thundered away, the old man's body lay motionless in the dirt, blood pooling beneath him and soaking into the dry earth. The scarred man didn't look back. For him, it was just another loose end tied off—and one step closer to disappearing with the gold.

CHAPTER ONE

The afternoon sun bore down on the dusty streets of Ironwood, casting long shadows against the worn wooden storefronts. Nash shifted in his saddle as his mare plodded along, her hooves kicking up small puffs of dirt. His wide-brimmed hat shielded his face, but not enough to block the heat that clung to the air. It had been a long ride, and the promise of a warm meal and a decent bed lured him forward like an oasis in the desert.

Ironwood was small, even by frontier standards. A single main street cut through the town, flanked by a handful of businesses—a livery stable, a general store, a barber, and the Ironwood Saloon, its weathered sign creaking on rusted hinges. Nash scanned the scene, taking in the subdued bustle of townsfolk moving about. They seemed tense, their conversations clipped, their eyes darting toward him before quickly looking away. Trouble had passed through this place recently, and it left its mark.

Nash tugged gently on the reins, bringing his mare to a stop in front of the saloon. He swung down from the saddle, boots crunching against the packed dirt, and tied his horse to the hitching post. With a practiced motion, he adjusted his hat and dusted off his coat before stepping onto the creaking wooden porch.

The saloon door swung open with a groan, and the atmosphere inside hit him like a wall. The place was dimly lit, the air thick with the scent of stale beer and tobacco. A few patrons sat at scattered tables, their conversations dropping to hushed murmurs as Nash entered. The bartender, a short, squat man with a bushy mustache, paused mid-swipe of a glass to give him a once-over. Nash ignored the stares, moving to the bar with the steady gait of a man used to such scrutiny.

"Whiskey," Nash said, his voice low and even.

The bartender, a wiry man with a salt-and-pepper beard and tired eyes, barely glanced up from wiping the counter. "The Dusty Trail's a two-bit saloon, cowboy," he muttered, his tone flat, as if warning Nash not to expect much.

Nash's eyes swept the room, taking in the scene. It sure didn't look like a two-bit saloon—not by a long shot. The floor was scuffed and uneven, years of boot heels and spilt liquor etched into the worn planks. The bar top had seen better days, its surface pitted and stained, the brass footrail tarnished. A few battered tables leaned precariously, surrounded by rough-looking patrons nursing drinks that were probably more water than whiskey. The piano in the corner had keys missing, and the tinny clang of the out-of-tune melody it had played earlier still hung in the air.

Nash didn't argue. He'd been in worse places, and he wasn't here for the decor. Without a word, he reached into his jacket and pulled out two coins, placing them on the bar with a soft clink. With a steady hand, he slid them toward the bartender, his eyes cool and unreadable.

The bartender eyed the coins, then, with a grunt, he pocketed them and reached for a bottle, the liquid inside sloshing with a dull thud as he poured.
Nash lifted the glass to his lips, the whiskey biting on the way down—harsh, cheap, and exactly what he expected. He set the glass down, sliding it back toward the bartender. "If this is two-bit whiskey," he said, his voice edged with dry amusement, "you boys are gettin' robbed."

The bartender huffed through his nose, the closest thing to a laugh Nash figured he'd get. "You want better, ride to Dallas," he said, moving away to tend to another customer.
Nash rested his elbows on the bar, letting the liquor settle in his gut as he took another slow look around the room. The place was rough, full of men who had seen too many hard days and not enough good

ones. The shuffle of cards, the low murmur of conversation, and the occasional clatter of a chair filled the space, but Nash didn't pay it much mind.

He took another slow sip of the whiskey, letting the burn settle in his chest. "Quiet town," Nash said, glancing at the bartender.

The man grunted, his mustache twitching. "Quiet most days. Today's different."

Nash raised an eyebrow. "How so?"

The bartender hesitated, his eyes flicking toward a group of men at a nearby table. They were rough-looking, their clothes dusty, and their hands resting a little too close to their holstered guns. One of them caught Nash's gaze and sneered before turning back to his companions.

"There was trouble this morning," the bartender said confidentially, his voice barely carrying over the hum of the saloon. He leaned closer, his expression grim. "Bank got hit. Ugly business."

Nash tilted his head slightly, his fingers tracing idle patterns on the counter. "Who was involved?"

The bartender wiped a glass absently, glancing over his shoulder as if to check who might be listening. "Dan Eldon, a big rancher from out past the river—took a bullet. Dead on the spot. His family's stirrin' up somethin' fierce, cryin' for blood."

Nash's brow furrowed, but he said nothing, letting the man continue.

"And then there's poor Donkey Sam," the bartender added, his tone dropping lower. "Harmless old fella just happened to be on the street when the gang rode out. Caught a stray. Didn't stand a chance."

Nash's jaw tightened. "Any leads on the gang?"

The bartender shook his head. "Not much, just that they were fast and mean. Folks reckon they're holed up somewhere nearby, but the sheriff's got no real direction. Lotta folks think it might've been one of those gangs passin' through. Still... with Eldon gone, this town's about to turn into a powder keg."

Nash set his glass down, his fingers sliding two more coins across the bar. "Another, if you will."

The bartender snorted, wiping the rim of a dirty glass with the same rag he'd been using all night. "Didn't figure you liked it," he said, eyeing Nash with a hint of amusement.

Nash leaned slightly on the bar, his expression unreadable. "Well, unless you've got anything else," he replied, his voice smooth but edged with a challenge.

The bartender chuckled dryly, shaking his head as he reached for the bottle. "Ain't nobody in here drinkin' for the taste," he muttered, pouring another measure of the amber liquid into Nash's glass. "They drink 'cause it's wet, and it burns going down."

Nash picked up the glass, turning it slowly in his hand, the lamplight catching in the whiskey's dull glow. He took a sip, letting it sit on his tongue for a moment before swallowing. It burned, alright—like swallowing a campfire and regret all at once.

He set the glass back down and gave the bartender a long look. "Ain't that the truth."

The bartender grinned, and then the smile fell from his face as the saloon doors banged open, and a heavyset man in a dusty coat strode in. The newcomer stood near the doorway, his stance casual but carrying an unmistakable air of authority. His duster coat hung open and on his chest, and the silver from the star he wore caught the dim light. The coat was hitched back slightly on one side, ensuring everyone had a clear view of the well-worn revolver resting easily in the holster strapped low on his hip.

His fingers hovered close to it, not in a threatening way, but in the kind of practiced ease that spoke of years of knowing when to use it. The scuffed leather of his gun belt was molded to his frame, each loop holding extra rounds, and the grip of his Colt showed the smooth wear of a weapon that had seen plenty of action.

His eyes, sharp and assessing, moved slowly around the room, taking in the crowd with the kind of gaze that made men straighten their backs and think twice about whatever trouble they were brewing. The lines around his mouth were deep-set, the kind that came from equal parts worry and experience, and when his gaze landed on Nash, there was no mistaking the weight behind it.

Without a word, the sheriff stepped forward, the creak of his boots on the uneven saloon floor the only sound. The conversation had died the moment he had entered with his deputies. The air thickened, tension riding along with him like an unwelcome companion. Behind him stood two deputies, hovering expectantly, waiting for instructions.

The room fell silent, all eyes on the newcomers. The sheriff's gaze swept the room before landing on Nash. His expression darkened.

"You there," the sheriff barked, pointing a thick finger. "What's your name?"

Nash turned slowly, his expression unreadable. "Depends who's askin'."

The sheriff stalked forward, his boots thudding against the wooden floor. "Sheriff

Bill Anders. Now, I'll ask again. What's your name?"

"Nash," he said simply, his tone steady.

"Just Nash?" the sheriff pressed, his eyes narrowing.

"That's all you need," Nash replied.

The sheriff studied him for a moment, his jaw tightening. "Where were you this morning?"

"On the trail," Nash said, his voice calm but firm. "Rode in from the south. Got here about ten minutes ago."

The sheriff glanced at his deputies, who exchanged uneasy looks. "Funny thing, Nash. A couple of witnesses said they saw a drifter riding out of town after the robbery. Said he looked a lot like you. Said they saw the same man coming into the saloon not ten minutes ago."

Nash's eyes flicked to the sheriff, his jaw tightening slightly. "I reckon you've got the wrong man."

The sheriff wasn't convinced. "We'll see about that. Boys, take his gun."

One of the deputies stepped forward, hand outstretched. Nash's hand hovered near his Colt, but he stopped himself, knowing this wasn't the time to make a stand. He unbuckled his gun belt slowly and held it out, his movements slow and deliberate.

"Smart move," the sheriff said, taking a step back. "Now, let's go. You're coming with us."

"For what?" Nash asked, his voice laced with quiet defiance.

"Questionin'," the sheriff said bluntly.

The deputies didn't wait, one on either side, they grabbed Nash by the arms, their grips firm but wary. Nash didn't resist, he knew that was pointles, and he let them lead him out of the saloon. The patrons watched in silence, their faces a mix of curiosity and unease.

As they stepped into the street, the sun blazed overhead, casting harsh shadows across the buildings. A small crowd had gathered, their murmurs growing louder as Nash was marched from the saloon and out toward the jailhouse. They'd obviously heard ahead of time that there was about to be an arrest. The tension was palpable, the weight of their suspicion pressing down on him like a physical force.

The jailhouse was a squat, weather-beaten building with iron bars on the windows. Inside, the air was stifling, the scent of sweat and damp wood thick in the air. The deputies shoved Nash into a cell, slamming the door shut behind him.

"Make yourself comfortable," the sheriff said, his tone dripping with sarcasm. "You're gonna be here awhile."

Nash didn't respond. He moved to the narrow cot in the corner and sat down, his expression unreadable. He listened as the sheriff and his deputies moved to the front office, their voices low and conspiratorial.

Leaning back against the wall, Nash let out a slow breath. He wasn't sure how he was going to get out of this mess, but one thing was certain—he wasn't going to hang for someone else's crime.

CHAPTER TWO

The night had barely settled over Ironwood when the first shouts split the uneasy quiet, raw and angry, echoing through the narrow streets like a war cry. Nash sat on the edge of the cot in the cramped jail cell, his muscles tensing at the rising commotion outside. The voices were thick with fury, swelling like a tide as more people flooded the street.

"Bring him out!" a voice bellowed, sharp with the kind of righteous anger that couldn't be reasoned with. "We'll see justice done tonight!"

Nash rose from the cot and moved to the barred window, peering out into the murky darkness. Torchlight flickered wildly, casting restless shadows that stretched long across the dusty street. The crowd outside was swelling, their faces hard and set in grim determination. Ranch hands with dirt-streaked clothes and dust-scuffed boots stood shoulder to shoulder with shopkeepers in worn aprons, their fists clenched tight; plenty carried rifles and revolvers. A few women stood among them, their expressions cold, their eyes reflecting the firelight like distant stars. At the front, a wiry man with a grizzled beard spat onto the ground, his mouth twisted in a snarl. Nash could see the rage in their eyes—the kind that came from grief and the need for vengeance.

On the wooden porch of the jailhouse, Sheriff Anders stood tall, his broad silhouette outlined against the dim glow spilling from the doorway. His hat sat low over his brow, casting a shadow across his face, but Nash didn't need to see his eyes to know he was tense. Two deputies flanked him, their hands gripping rifles with knuckles white against the wood, their faces drawn tight with unease.

"Y'all need to turn around and head home," Anders called, his voice even but edged with warning. "This ain't how we do things in Ironwood."

"How else are we supposed to do it, Sheriff?" a thick-set rancher shouted from the middle of the mob, his voice sharp and laced with accusation. "That drifter fits the damn description! Dan Eldon was shot down in cold blood right on the bank steps! You expect us to sit and do nothin'?"

A chorus of agreement roared through the crowd, fists rising in the air, the collective weight of their anger pressing in on the jailhouse walls like a physical force.

Inside, Nash felt the weight of their hatred settling like a stone in his gut. He stepped back from the window, his fists clenching. He'd been here before, and he knew how these things went. The only thing more dangerous than a guilty man was an angry mob looking for a scapegoat.

"Hell of a town," he muttered under his breath, running a hand through his dusty hair.

In the front room, Anders' boots paced heavy against the wooden planks. Nash could hear the sharp edge to his voice, though he tried to keep it steady. "We don't know if he did it," Anders snapped to his deputies. "No evidence, no trial, and I'm not handing him over to be strung up without proof."

"You think they care about proof?" one of the deputies shot back, his voice tight with fear. "They want blood, Sheriff, and they want it tonight."

Nash pressed his fingers against the bridge of his nose. The knots in his stomach twisted tighter. He'd seen frontier justice before—quick, merciless, and almost always wrong. He sank back onto the cot, letting out a slow breath. The bed creaked under his weight, but the sound was drowned out by the mounting chaos outside.

Suddenly, the sharp crack of shattering glass echoed through the jailhouse. A rock sailed through one of the small front windows, scattering shards across the wooden floor. The Sheriff cursed under his breath.

Anders stormed out onto the porch, raising his rifle high, his voice booming. "Get back! I'm warnin' you now! Anyone who crosses that line gets locked up!"

"Maybe it's you who needs lockin' up, Anders!" a woman shouted, her voice shrill with fury. "You ain't done a damn thing for this town!"

They pressed forwards, angry and intent on revenge, they wanted to make it inside the jailhouse. Tension snapped like a wire stretched far too tight. One of the deputies, his nerves shot, raised his rifle and fired a shot into the air in an attempt to stop them from pressing forward. The blast echoed off the buildings, momentarily silencing the crowd. Faces flickered with hesitation, but it didn't last long. The roar rose again, louder, angrier, the scent of torches and sweat thick in the night air.

Inside the cell, Nash listened intently. He could hear it—the Sheriff's bravado, strong but brittle. Anders was standing firm for now, but Nash knew it wouldn't take much for the scales to tip the other way. The town's grief, their need for revenge, was stronger than any badge.

Outside, the situation was only getting worse. The mob of townsfolk were pressing closer, restless and their anger was ready to spill over. The Sheriff's grip on his rifle tightened. This wasn't just a town looking for justice anymore; this was a storm ready to break, and Nash had found himself right slap-bang in the middle of it.

The sound of hooves in the distance cut through the noise. They were faint at first, but steadily, they were growing louder. Nash froze, his instincts prickling.

The night air was thick with tension, the kind that settled deep into a man's bones. The shouts outside the jailhouse had grown louder and angrier, and Nash could hear the restless murmur of the crowd gathering in the street. He sat on the edge of the narrow cot in his cell, his jaw tight, listening to the telltale creak of wood as boots paced outside. The flicker of torches threw wild shadows through the barred window, painting jagged shapes across the walls.

The pounding on the jailhouse door came again, harder this time. "Anders! Bring him out!" a voice roared. "Dan Eldon's blood needs settlin', and we ain't waitin' no more!"

Sheriff Anders stood near the front door, his shoulders squared, rifle resting in his hands. His deputies, Franklin and Miller, exchanged nervous glances, their hands hovering near their holsters. The tension in the room was thick enough to choke on.

"Stay calm," Anders muttered to them, his voice low but firm. "Ain't gonna be no lynchin' on my watch."

From his cell, Nash could see the Sheriff's jaw working, the tight set of his mouth betraying his concern. He knew Anders was a man of the law, but the crowd outside wasn't interested in justice. They wanted blood—his blood.

The voice outside grew sharper, more insistent. "That drifter fits the description! We all saw it! My pa's dead, and you're protectin' the cur who killed him!"

Nash leaned against the bars, his gaze locking onto Anders. "You know I didn't kill Dan Eldon," he said evenly, his voice cutting through the tension like a knife.

Anders' grip on his rifle tightened, but he didn't look at Nash. "It ain't about what I know," he muttered. "It's about what they believe."

Another heavy thud hit the door, shaking it on its hinges. A rock smashed through the window, sending glass skittering across the floor. Franklin swore under his breath, stepping back from the door.

"They're gonna come through that door any second, Sheriff," Nash said, watching the crowd swell outside. "And if they do, you're gonna have a hell of a mess on your hands."

Anders let out a slow breath, his eyes flicking toward his deputies. "Franklin," he said, "get him out the back. Take him to the edge of town. Make sure he doesn't come back till this blows over."

Franklin's eyes widened. "You sure about that, Sheriff? What if they find out?"

"Just do it," Anders snapped. "We're running out of time."

Nash smirked faintly as Franklin fumbled with the keys, his hands shaking as he unlocked the cell door. "Move," the deputy muttered, shoving Nash toward the back door.

The cool night air hit him like a slap as they stepped into the alley behind the jailhouse. The noise of the mob was muffled now, but Nash could still hear the angry roar beyond the thick walls. He took a few steps before turning sharply, driving his elbow hard into Franklin's gut. The deputy doubled over with a grunt, and before he could recover, Nash caught him with a swift blow to the jaw, sending him crumpling to the ground.

"Sorry, kid," Nash muttered, kneeling to pull the deputy's revolver from his belt. He checked the chamber—four rounds left. It would have to do.

With the gun tucked into his belt, Nash slipped to the hitching post where his mare was still tied. He swung into the saddle, casting a quick glance back at the jailhouse. The door was rattling now, the wood splintering under the force of the crowd's fury. He could hear the Eldon boys shouting, their anger burning hotter with every second.

"You're in for a long night, Sheriff," Nash murmured under his breath. He dug his heels into the mare's sides, and she bolted into the darkness.

As he rode out of Ironwood, the shouts and flickering torches faded behind him. But Nash knew this wasn't over. Not by a long shot. The dust trailing behind him carried more than the weight of his escape—it carried the promise of unfinished business.

CHAPTER THREE

Nash rode hard, his mare's hooves drumming a frantic rhythm against the hard-packed earth, each stride kicking up clouds of dust that vanished into the night. The town of Ironwood faded behind him, swallowed by the darkness, but the echoes of the mob still rang in his ears. His pulse was hammering in time with the steady gallop. He pushed her on, knowing they'd be looking for him—angry men with torches and bullets, eager to see him swinging from a rope.

The chill of the desert night seeped into his bones as he rode, the sweat from his earlier escape drying cold against his skin. The vast openness of the plains stretched out ahead, but he wasn't fool enough to stay in the open. He needed cover. Shelter. Somewhere to catch his breath.

An hour passed before he finally spotted the jagged silhouette of a canyon cutting through the land. He pulled back on the reins, slowing his mare to a trot, her flanks heaving from the run. "Easy, girl," he muttered, his voice rough with exhaustion. He guided her into the mouth of the canyon, the towering rock walls rising up around them, a protective cloak against the moonlight. It was a tight fit, the walls pressing close, but it would do. If anyone came hunting, they'd have to work hard to find him.

Nash slid down from the saddle, landing with a grunt and patting the mare's damp neck. "You did good," he murmured, running a hand down her trembling flank. The mare snorted, her warm breath misting in the cool air. She was spent, and so was he.

He tugged the deputy's revolver from his belt, turning it over in his hand. The iron was cold, the grip worn smooth from years of use. He popped the cylinder open and spun it, counting the bullets—five rounds, one empty chamber resting beneath the hammer. Smart move, kid, Nash thought grimly. He snapped the cylinder shut and gave the gun a quick test, feeling the weight, the balance. It wasn't his gun, but it was better than nothing.

His gaze drifted down to his empty saddle, frustration gnawing at him. No rifle. No knife. No saddlebags filled with supplies. Everything he owned was still back in Ironwood, likely dumped out and picked through by now. His fingers curled around the revolver tighter. He had nothing but the clothes on his back, the mare under him, and a six-shooter with five bullets.

His stomach grumbled low, reminding him of just how little he had. No food, no water, no matches to build a fire. He grimaced, pushing the hunger aside. He'd gone without before. He could do it again.

He led the mare deeper into the canyon, finding a small patch of scrub where she could graze. Tying her to a low branch, he rubbed her down with his hands, brushing away the dust and sweat from their hard ride. "Rest up," he murmured. "We'll move again soon." The mare flicked an ear but stood quiet, her eyes watching him in the dim light.

Nash crouched down by the canyon wall, resting his back against the cool stone. He pulled his hat lower over his eyes, listening to the wind as it whispered through the rocks. Somewhere in the distance, a coyote let out a mournful howl, the sound carrying far across the open land.

He sighed, pulling the revolver from his belt again and setting it in his lap. His fingers traced the worn grip absently as his mind worked through his next move. He couldn't stay here long. The Eldon boys wouldn't give up easily, and once they realized he was gone, they'd be scouring the hills and canyons like bloodhounds.

He reached into his coat pocket, finding nothing but a few loose coins and a folded scrap of paper. Sadie's last letter was creased and worn from being read too many times. Nash rubbed a thumb over it, the familiar loop of her handwriting a stark contrast to the rough world he lived in. How long had it been since he'd seen her? His mind handed him an instant answer – a month. But Nash knew it was wrong, more like six, but he preferred not to think about it. He'd left it too long, and he knew it. Roughly he pushed the letter back into his pocket – out of mind.

A sharp crack echoed through the canyon, and Nash tensed, his grip tightening on the gun. He held his breath, listening. The mare shifted uneasily, ears flicking in different directions. Nash remained still, straining to catch any sound beyond the soft rustle of the wind and the distant howl of the coyote.

Nothing.

After a long moment, he let out the breath he'd been holding, his shoulders easing slightly. He couldn't afford to spook himself. Not yet. He closed his eyes for a moment, exhaustion weighing heavy, but sleep wouldn't come easy. Not out here, not with a price on his head and a town full of men eager to collect it.

The canyon walls loomed around him, cold and unyielding, but for now, they were his only friends. He settled in, gripping the revolver tightly, and let the darkness of the night take him.

Nash sagged against the rough canyon wall, every muscle in his body protesting as exhaustion settled deep in his bones. The ride out of Ironwood had been hard, every pounding hoofbeat a reminder of how close he'd come to ending up at the wrong end of a noose. His mind was running in overdrive, cycling through the last few hours in a relentless loop.

The mob outside the sheriff's office, their faces twisted with anger and grief. The shouting and the torches cast wild shadows across the jail's walls. Anders stood firm on that rickety porch, trying to hold them off with nothing but his badge and a stubborn sense of justice. And then the escape—Franklin's startled expression right before Nash's elbow sent him sprawling into the dirt. He didn't regret it. Better the deputy woke up with a sore head than Nash waking up at the end of a rope.

With a slow, careful breath, he shifted his position against the canyon wall, trying to find some measure of comfort. The stone was cool against his back, grounding him in the moment. He needed a plan—needed it yesterday—but his mind was too tired to think straight.

The situation was worse than he'd thought. It wasn't just the Eldon boys out for blood; the whole damn town wanted him dead. And without his saddlebags, without food, water, or even a match to light a fire, survival was looking like a mean son of a bitch.

The mare snorted softly a few feet away, the sound grounding him in the stillness. Nash listened to her steady breathing, the occasional rustle of her shifting hooves in the gravel. At least she was here. That was something. He reached out, resting a hand lightly on her flank, feeling the warmth of her beneath his palm. "You've done good, girl," he murmured, his voice low and rough. The horse flicked an ear in response but didn't stir

He tugged the deputy's revolver from his belt, turning it over in his hands with practiced ease. The weight of it felt unfamiliar, off-balance compared to his own Colt, but it was better than nothing. He rotated the cylinder, making sure a live round sat under the hammer before snapping it shut with a quiet click.

A coyote yipped somewhere in the distance, its lonely cry carrying through the canyon. Nash's gaze drifted upward to the sliver of sky visible between the jagged rock walls. The stars were out, sharp and bright, indifferent to the trouble churning below them. He envied them their distance.

Letting out a slow breath, he forced his eyes shut, his grip on the revolver loosening just enough to keep his fingers from locking up. Sleep wouldn't come easy. He told himself he'd rest for an hour—just enough to let the ache in his bones settle, just enough to keep his strength up for whatever came next.

The night pressed in around him, heavy and still. He let it wrap around him, a temporary reprieve from the dangers lurking beyond the canyon walls. Tomorrow would bring more trouble—he could feel it hanging in the air like an approaching storm—but for now, he'd take what little peace he could find.

CHAPTER FOUR

The first pale streaks of dawn were creeping over the horizon when Nash opened his eyes.. He lay still for a moment, listening to the quiet rustling of the wind through the brush and the distant cry of a coyote. It was a rare moment of peace, but it didn't last long—his mind was already working.

He needed a plan.

Tracking down Slade's gang was the only way he'd clear his name and put an end to this mess. The thought of leaving Ironwood behind and letting them get away didn't sit right with him. They'd left a trail of bodies, and if they weren't stopped, there'd be more. Nash wasn't about to let that happen—not with his name still tied to their crimes.

"Alright," he muttered to himself, running a hand over his stubbled jaw. "First things first."

He was going to have to double back and pick up the trail, piece it together like he had done a dozen times before. Slade and his boys weren't the kind to cover their tracks too carefully; from what he'd heard, they'd left in a hurry; they relied on speed and fear to keep anyone from following. But Nash knew the land, and he knew how outlaws thought. If he could get to where they split off from town, he could follow their trail—slow, steady, and relentless.

It wasn't much of a plan, but it was better than none.

All he had to do was find it.

He rode in silence, keeping his senses sharp, scanning the ground for signs of passage—hoof prints, broken brush, anything out of place. The early morning sun cast long shadows across the landscape, revealing the faint traces of churned-up dirt where riders had passed through not long ago. Nash reined in his mare and leaned down, studying the trail.

A scattering of hoofprints—too many to be a single rider, too erratic to be a cattle drive.

Nash smirked. "Gotcha," he muttered, following the tracks northward.

It was slow going, but Nash was patient. The trail led him through narrow passes and dry creek beds, each step forward peeling back the story of the gang's flight. Occasionally, he dismounted to study deeper impressions, noting where they had rested their horses or where they'd veered off to avoid a more visible path.

They were headed toward the hills.

By midday, Nash had a solid sense of their direction. He wiped the sweat from his brow, his mind ticking over what came next. He'd have to be careful. A cornered outlaw was the most dangerous kind, and Slade wouldn't take kindly to being hunted down.

But Nash had no intention of turning back now.

He set his sights on the distant hills, nudged his mare into motion, and rode on, the wind carrying the promise of trouble ahead. The sun burned its slow descent across the sky, stretching the shadows and bathing the rugged land in a wash of gold and crimson. Nash followed the trail with the patience of a hunter. The tracks wound through dry gullies and across rocky ridges, sometimes disappearing for a while before revealing themselves again in the soft earth near the occasional watering hole.

He pulled his mare to a stop atop a rise, looking out over the landscape with a practiced eye. The hills ahead were dark against the setting sun, their jagged peaks and deep ravines promising both shelter and danger. He could feel it in his gut—Slade and his men were out there, holed up somewhere in the labyrinth of canyons, waiting for the heat to die down.

Nash let out a slow breath, wiping the sweat from his brow. His stomach gnawed at him. But food would have to wait. He studied the trail ahead, noting the way it disappeared into the hills, then glanced up at the sky.

The sun was dipping low now, streaking the heavens with shades of amber and deep violet. It wouldn't be long before the darkness swallowed the landscape whole, and Nash knew better than to stumble around unfamiliar terrain at night. He pulled the reins, guiding his mare toward a small outcropping of boulders nestled in the lee of a rocky bluff. It would offer some shelter from the wind and, more importantly, keep him out of sight.

Dismounting with a weary grunt, Nash loosened the girth on his saddle and gave his mare an affectionate pat. "Rest up, girl," he murmured, slipping the bridle from her mouth and letting her graze on the sparse patches of grass. He crouched near the base of the bluff, scanning the horizon one last time before settling in.

The ground was hard and unforgiving beneath him, but Nash had known worse. He leaned back against the rock, feeling the day's ride settle into his bones. The distant howl of a coyote echoed through the hills, followed by the answering call of another. Nash smirked to himself—if the coyotes were out, at least he knew Slade's men weren't close enough to spook them.

Nash pulled his coat tighter, staring up at the darkening sky. The stars were beginning to blink into view, tiny pinpricks against the vast, endless black.

He could feel the weight of the past days pressing down on him—Ironwood, the jail, the beating from the Eldon boys, and now the relentless chase across the unforgiving terrain. For a moment, he let his eyes close, listening to the whisper of the wind through the canyon and the occasional snort from his mare.

But sleep didn't come easy, not when he was this close.

His mind kept turning over the possibilities—where the gang might be holed up, how many men were left, and just how deep this trouble ran. The sheriff would be gathering a posse soon enough, but Nash had no intention of waiting around.

The crackle of a twig snapped Nash back to the present. His hand instinctively drifted to the Colt on his hip as his eyes scanned the darkness. A breeze stirred the dry grass, and Nash watched, waiting. Nothing. Just the wind playing tricks on his tired mind.

He sighed, shifting on the ground and staring back up at the stars. "One more day," he muttered to himself. "Then I find 'em."

With that, he closed his eyes again, forcing his body to relax. Tomorrow, the hunt would begin in earnest. Tonight, he'd take what rest he could get.

The following morning, the wilderness stretched in every direction, an endless expanse of dry scrub and jagged rock formations that jutted up like the bones of some ancient beast. The land was harsh and unforgiving, a place where only the hardiest souls could carve out an existence. Nash had spent enough time in a country like this to know its rhythms—the way the wind danced through the mesquite, the rustle of distant wildlife, the crunch of his mare's hooves against the parched earth. But today, the silence felt heavier, thick with something unspoken. It was the kind of quiet that warned a man to stay sharp.

Nash shifted in the saddle, his gaze sweeping the horizon. The morning sun had begun its slow climb, casting long, wavering shadows across the landscape, turning the sagebrush into dark, spectral figures. His mind turned over the events of the past few days—the bank robbery, the angry mob in Ironwood that had nearly put him in the ground. He wasn't out of danger yet.

The trail beneath him wound through rocky outcrops and clusters of gnarled juniper trees, their twisted limbs stretching toward the sky like desperate hands. He nudged his mare forward, letting her pick her way carefully through the terrain. The wind carried the distant cry of a hawk, high and lonesome, and for a brief moment, Nash felt like the only soul left in the world.

Then his mare snorted, ears flicking forward sharply. Nash tightened his grip on the reins, his body tensing instinctively. "Easy now," he muttered under his breath, patting her neck. She was a good horse, smart and reliable, and she never spooked without reason. He pulled her to a halt, his eyes narrowing as he scanned the landscape ahead. The wind shifted slightly, and that's when he caught it—a thin, curling column of smoke rising into the sky from beyond a nearby ridge.

Smoke. Someone was out here.

His hand drifted to the worn grip of the Colt resting against his hip, his fingers brushing the smooth steel. He remained still for a long moment, watching the smoke curl lazily into the morning air. It could be just another traveler passing through. It could also be worse.

Taking a deep breath, Nash clicked his tongue and urged his mare forward at a slow, cautious pace. The dry earth crunched softly beneath her hooves, muffled by the sandy path as he wound his way toward the source of the smoke. The landscape shifted subtly, the ground sloping downward into a shallow ravine carved out by long-dry seasonal rains. The campfire came into view first, a small flicker of orange and red nestled in the shelter of the rocky walls.

Near the fire, a lone figure crouched, tending to something in a battered tin pot. Nash slowed his approach, keeping his mare just inside the tree line where the shadows were thick. He studied the figure, taking in the details. A wide-brimmed hat tilted low over the face. A dust-covered duster hung loosely over their shoulders, the fabric worn thin at the edges. The pants, scuffed and patched, told a story of hard travel. But what caught Nash's attention most was the rifle propped against a nearby rock, positioned just within easy reach.

Whoever they were, they were no stranger to trouble.

Nash watched for a moment longer, noting the way the figure moved—deliberate but unhurried, like someone who wasn't expecting company but wouldn't be caught off guard if it came. The fire crackled softly, sending occasional sparks spiraling into the morning breeze, and the scent of coffee mingled with the woodsmoke, curling into Nash's nostrils. His stomach growled, reminding him that he hadn't eaten, but hunger was the least of his concerns.

He eased his mare forward another few steps, clearing his throat to announce his presence. The figure stiffened immediately, one hand instinctively going to their side while the other remained near the rifle. Nash raised his free hand slowly, keeping his tone calm but firm.

"Morning," he called out. "Didn't mean to startle you."

The figure turned slightly, and beneath the brim of the hat, a pair of sharp, assessing eyes met his. A woman. Her expression was hard and unreadable, but Nash didn't miss the way her shoulders tensed like a coiled spring ready to snap.

"You always sneak up on folks?" she asked, her voice dry and even; the duster coat was hitched back over the revolver at her hip.

"Only when I ain't sure how friendly they are," Nash replied, keeping his tone light.

The woman's gaze flicked to his holstered Colt, then back to his face. "Friendly enough if you don't give me a reason otherwise."

Nash gave a slow nod, dismounting carefully but keeping his hands in plain sight. He studied her closer now. Her face was lean, sun-worn, and marked by a few faint scars that suggested she'd seen her fair share of scrapes. Her hair was tucked beneath her hat, but strands of auburn curled loosely at the nape of her neck. Despite her rough appearance, there was a sharpness in her eyes—intelligence and wariness in equal measure.

"Looks like you've been out here a while," Nash said, taking a step closer to the fire. "Mind if I sit for a spell?"

She considered him for a long moment, her fingers still close to the rifle. Finally, she gave a curt nod. "Suit yourself. Fire's warm, coffee's hot."

Nash eased himself down onto a nearby rock. He watched as she poured a measure of coffee into a chipped tin cup and handed it over without a word. He accepted it, taking a careful sip, letting the warmth settle in his gut.

"Name's Nash," he offered, setting the cup down.

She didn't answer right away, stirring the pot with a slow, deliberate motion. "Willa," she said finally. "What brings you out here, Nash?"

Nash smirked, leaning back slightly. "Long story." His eyes flicked to the rifle again. "What about you?"

Willa shrugged, her lips curving in the faintest of smiles. "I ain't much for stories."

Nash chuckled, taking another sip of the strong, bitter coffee. Something told him this woman had plenty of stories to tell—if he could get her to trust him enough to share them. But for now, he'd settle for the coffee and the fire.

"So, what are you doing on my trail?" she said, her voice low and steady. There was no mistaking the warning in her tone.

Nash tilted his head, studying her. "Didn't know it was your trail. I saw the smoke and thought I'd check it out."

"Right," she said, her lips twitching into a faint smirk. "A lone rider just happens to stumble on my camp. Pull the other one."

He held up his hands, palms out. "I'm tracking a gang that hit Ironwood a few days back."

Her expression didn't change, but Nash saw the flicker of recognition in her eyes. "Ironwood," she repeated, her tone neutral. She glanced past him, scanning the trail he'd come from before focusing on him again. "And why would you be doing that?"

"Got accused of ridin' with them," Nash replied evenly. "Figured the best way to clear my name was to find the real culprits."

Her gaze narrowed. "Convenient story."

"It's the truth," Nash said. He nodded toward her rifle. "What about you? You seem pretty comfortable out here?"

The smirk returned, sharper this time. "Willa Callahan," she said, tipping her hat slightly. "And you're right. I'm tracking the same gang. They've got a price on their heads from here to the state line, leader's a mean son-of-gun called Slade."

Nash raised an eyebrow. "Then I reckon we've got the same goal."

"Maybe," Willa said, her voice laced with skepticism. She stepped closer, her boots crunching against the dirt. "But I've been at this long enough to know better than to trust some drifter who just shows up on my doorstep. How do I know you're not one of them?"

"You don't," Nash admitted. "But if I was, you think I'd ride in here alone and unannounced?"

Willa's eyes flicked over him, taking in the worn duster, the dust-caked boots, and the revolver on his hip. She didn't say anything for a long moment, and Nash got the impression she was weighing her options.

"So," she said, leaning against a tree, "tell me what you know about this gang."

"They hit the Ironwood Savings Bank," Nash said. "Killed a couple folks and made off with the contents of the safe.

Sheriff thinks they've holed up somewhere in the hills."

Willa nodded slowly. "That fits. I've been trailing them for weeks. They've got a pattern—small towns, big hauls, and a lot of bodies left behind."

"Sounds like you've been busy," Nash said.

Her expression hardened. "Busy doesn't cover it. These bastards hit a stagecoach outside Miltonville three months back. Killed everyone on board. I knew people on there, good people who didn't deserve to die."

The weight of her words hung heavy in the air. Nash nodded, his respect for her growing. "Sorry to hear that."

Willa shrugged, though the pain in her eyes was unmistakable. "Don't need your pity. Just need them dead."

"Fair enough," Nash said. He leaned forward slightly. "Look, I don't know you, and you don't know me. But we're both after the same thing. Maybe it makes sense to work together."

Her eyes narrowed. "And why should I trust you?"

"Because you're smart enough to know you'll need help when you catch up to them," Nash said. "And because I've got a knack for finding people who don't want to be found."

Willa studied him for a long moment, her expression unreadable. Finally, she sighed and shook her head. "Alright, Nash. You're in. But let me make one thing clear—if you so much as look like you're about to cross me, I'll put a bullet between your eyes."

"Noted," Nash said, a faint smile tugging at the corner of his mouth.

Willa leaned against the side of her makeshift camp, arms crossed as her sharp eyes ran over Nash. Her gaze was calculating, taking in every detail like she was sizing him up for a fight—or a grave. No gun belt, just a revolver shoved into his waistband. No saddle bags, no bedroll. A man who looked like he'd been on the wrong side of luck and was barely hanging on.

"Is that all you got?" she asked, her voice flat, tinged with disbelief.

Nash shifted his weight, brushing the dust from his coat. "Had to leave in a hurry."

Willa's mouth pulled into something between a smirk and a frown. "Guessing you're hungry?"

"I'll settle with the coffee," Nash took another sip. It wasn't good, but it was hot, and right now, that was enough.

"Here," Willa leaned down, pulled out a tin of biscuits, and threw it towards him.

"I can hear your stomach complaining from here."

"Thankin' you kindly, ma'am," he said, catching the tin.

Her expression soured instantly. "Don't go ma'aming me," she snapped, her voice carrying a rough edge. "I ain't no lady."

Nash raised an eyebrow, unbothered by her tone. "No offense meant."

"Yeah, well, don't let it happen again," she growled back at him.

CHAPTER FIVE

The sun was low now, and the dimming light stretched the shadows of the trees across the narrow trail. The air was thick with the scent of pine and earth, mingling with the faint metallic tang of tension. Nash rode slightly ahead of Willa, his eyes scanning the path, every muscle in his body coiled for danger. Willa followed close behind, her rifle balanced across her lap, her sharp eyes darting to every shadow and movement.

As they rode in silence, Nash found himself stealing glances at Willa, taking the time to really study her for the first time. She rode with the easy confidence of someone who'd spent more time in the saddle than on solid ground, her posture relaxed but ready. Her face was sun-kissed, lightly dusted with freckles, and framed by short, unevenly cut hair that was more practical than fashionable. Beneath the brim of her battered hat, her eyes were a sharp, unwavering blue, scanning the terrain with a hunter's precision.

She wasn't like most women Nash had known. There was no pretense about her, no softness carefully put on to fool a man into thinking she needed protecting.

Willa was built, lean, and tough, her figure hidden beneath a well-worn duster that hung open just enough to reveal the holster strapped to her hip. She carried herself like someone who had been through more than her fair share of hard times and came out the other side stronger for it.

Her clothes, though practical, bore the marks of wear and hard use. Dust clung to the creases of her duster, and her boots, scuffed and worn, had seen many miles. The handle of her Colt was smooth from constant use, and Nash didn't doubt she knew how to use it. There was something in the way she moved—efficient, deliberate as if every step was calculated. She wasn't showy and didn't make a lot of noise, but there was a quiet deadliness about her that made it clear she was more than capable of holding her own.

Nash had known men who liked to underestimate women like Willa, but he wasn't that foolish. He turned his gaze back to the trail ahead, his thoughts stirring. Willa Callahan was an enigma, and Nash wasn't sure if that intrigued him or unsettled him. Either way, they were riding into trouble together, and he'd have to figure her out sooner or later.

They hadn't said much since breaking camp that morning, each absorbed in their own thoughts. Nash knew better than to let the silence fool him—Willa was as sharp as a blade, and she was watching him as much as she was the trail. But even her watchful eye couldn't shake the feeling crawling up his spine, like an itch just out of reach.

"Trail's too quiet," Willa muttered, her voice low. She'd pulled her horse up alongside Nash's, her lips pressed into a thin line.

Nash nodded, his hand brushing the Colt on his hip. "That's what's botherin' me."

The forest around them was dense, the trail winding through clusters of tall pines and jagged outcroppings of rock. It was the perfect spot for an ambush, and Nash didn't like being funneled through it with no clear line of sight.

"We keep ridin', or we turn back?" Willa asked, her voice for once serious and devoid of the sarcasm she usually wielded. This was her serious voice, and it only made the knot in Nash's gut tighten.

"Turnin' back makes us predictable," Nash said, his gaze fixed on the trail ahead. "We push through, but keep your eyes sharp. If they're out there, they're waitin' for us to let our guard down."

Willa didn't respond, her eyes on her rifle, checking it, her movements precise and practiced. Nash couldn't help but admire her composure, there was no outward ripple to betray any nerves at what they were about to do - her pa sure had taught her well. Although he knew better than to mention it. She wasn't the type to take compliments kindly.

As they rounded a bend, the first shot rang out.

It came from the trees, a sharp crack that shattered the silence. Nash's mare reared, startled, and Nash yanked the reins, pulling her back under control. Willa's horse sidestepped nervously, but she kept her seat with ease, her rifle already up and scanning the trees.

"Left!" Nash barked, his Colt level, he fired a shot toward the shadow of movement among the trees. The sudden harsh sound of a gunshot echoed through the forest, followed by another shot from their unseen attackers.

Willa dismounted in one fluid motion, dropping quickly to the ground, using her horse as cover. "They've got us pinned," she muttered, her voice calm despite the tension crackling in the air. She raised her rifle and fired, the sharp crack of the shot sending birds scattering from the treetops.

Nash slid from his saddle, his boots hitting the dirt with a dull thud. He crouched low, his Colt gripped tightly in his hand. "How many?"

"Three, maybe four," Willa replied, her eyes scanning the trees. "Could be more. Hard to tell with all this cover."

Another shot whizzed past, close enough that Nash felt the air move against his cheek. He ducked behind a fallen log, his heart pounding in his chest. "They're good," he muttered, peeking over the edge of the log to return fire. "Too good for this to be random."

Willa fired again, her shot answered by a yelp of pain from the trees. "That one won't be shootin' for a while," she said, a hint of satisfaction in her voice.

Nash smirked despite himself. "Not bad."

The exchange of gunfire continued, each shot a calculated gamble. Nash could feel the adrenaline surging through his veins, sharpening his senses. He moved carefully, using the terrain to his advantage, his mind racing to calculate angles and distances. He had four shots left, and he needed to make them count.

Willa moved like she'd been born to it, her rifle steady and her eyes cold and focused. She fired with precision, each shot deliberate. When she ran out of rounds, she reloaded with a speed that spoke of countless hours of practice.

"You alright over there?" Nash called out, his voice rising just enough to carry through the crack of gunfire and the snapping of the brush.

"Better than you," Willa shot back from her position, crouched low behind a rock. Her tone lacked malice, carrying a faint edge of amusement—or was it respect? "There's a box of rounds for your Colt in my pack if you can reach it."

Nash blinked, momentarily surprised. She'd noticed he was out of ammunition before. Smart, he thought, with a flicker of admiration. The gunfire ripped through the tension, and he ducked instinctively as another bullet chewed into the bark of a tree nearby.

"On my way," he called, making his decision.

Keeping low, Nash cut through the tangled brush, his shoulders hunched as another round whizzed overhead. His eyes were fastened onto Willa's horse, tied just out of the main line of fire, the pack strapped snugly against its flank. The animal snorted nervously, shifting its weight but staying put.

He reached the horse and crouched, one hand steadying the animal as his fingers worked at the leather straps. The knot was tight, and he cursed under his breath as bullets slammed into the dirt a few feet away. Finally, the strap gave way, and he yanked the pack free, slinging it over his shoulder.

A sharp crack sounded. The bullet struck a rock nearby, sending shards flying up into the air. Nash ducked, adrenaline coursing through him as he swung the pack open, searching quickly for the box of rounds. Finding them, his hands worked fast, snapping open the Colt's cylinder and feeding the cartridges into the empty chambers. Each quick click of a loaded round was a lifeline, the sound settling his nerves - now he had a chance.

Storing the remaining rounds in his coat pocket, Nash pivoted, keeping low as he scanned the landscape. Willa's position wasn't far—he could see the flash of her rifle as she fired off another shot, calm and steady.

"Got it!" he shouted, his voice rough.

Willa didn't reply immediately, but he caught a quick glance from her direction, the corner of her mouth pulling into a tight, approving smile before she turned back to the fight.

Nash took position behind a sturdy tree, lifting the freshly loaded Colt. He exhaled sharply, steadying his aim before firing off a precise shot that dropped one of the men closing in on their flank. Another outlaw ducked for cover, and Nash used the opening to pick off a second.

The balance of the fight shifted. With each shot, Nash pressed forward, matching Willa's steady rhythm of fire. Between them, the tide was turning, but Nash's thoughts kept circling back to her—quick-thinking, resourceful, and damn sharp-eyed.

As the chaos around them began to wane, Nash called out, his voice low but edged with respect. "Next time, don't wait so long to share your bullets."

Willa let out a dry laugh, a single shot dropping another man. "Figured I'd see if you were worth 'em first."

Nash smirked, shaking his head as he reloaded his Colt. "Guess I passed."

The attackers began to falter, their movements growing more erratic as Nash and Willa's relentless counterfire took its toll. Nash caught a glimpse of one of them—a wiry man with a bandana pulled over his face—breaking cover to move to a better position.

"They're fallin' back!" Willa yelled, firing another shot that ricocheted off a nearby tree. "Don't let 'em regroup!"

Nash ran forward, moving from cover to cover, keeping low, his Colt barking with each step. Another attacker dropped, clutching his side, and the remaining men scrambled to retreat, their confidence shattered.

The forest fell silent, the air thick with the smell of gunpowder and the faint echo of retreating footsteps. Nash straightened, his Colt still in hand, his eyes scanned the trees quickly for any sign of movement.

"You hurt?" he asked, glancing over at Willa.

She shook her head, lowering her rifle. "Not a scratch," she said, though her breathing was heavy, her chest rising and falling as the adrenaline began to fade.

Nash holstered his Colt, his gaze lingering on her for a moment. "You're one hell of a shot," he said, his tone carrying a rare note of respect, the compliment was genuininely made.

Willa smirked, wiping the sweat from her brow with the back of her hand. "Didn't think you'd notice, what with all your fancy gunplay."

Nash chuckled, shaking his head. "Fair's fair. You held your own out there."

The tension between them eased slightly, mutual respect settling in the air. Willa slung her rifle over her shoulder, her sharp eyes scanning the trees one last time. "Think they'll be back?"

"Not tonight," Nash said, his tone grim. "But this wasn't random. They were waitin' for us. They know we are on their trail. My guess is they left those men behind to deal with us."

Willa nodded her expression hard. "Then we'd better move. No tellin' how many more of 'em are out there."

CHAPTER SIX

They mounted up, their horses skittish but obedient, and rode deeper into the wilderness. The silence that followed was heavy, but it was no longer the uneasy silence of strangers. It was the silence of two people who had fought side by side and lived to tell the tale.

As they rode, Nash cast a sidelong glance at Willa. She was tough, no doubt about it. Tougher than most men he'd ridden with. And for the first time since this mess started, he felt a flicker of hope. Maybe, just maybe, they had a chance.

Later that evening Willa sat cross-legged on a rock near the campfire, her hat tipped back just enough to catch the glow of the flames on her face. She poked the embers with a stick, sending a shower of sparks spiraling into the night. Nash sat opposite her, his Colt resting within arm's reach, the silence between them unforced but heavy with unspoken questions.

"You're good with a gun," Nash finally said, his voice low. "Better than some men I've ridden with."

Willa snorted, a corner of her mouth twitching in a faint smile. "That so?" She didn't look up, keeping her focus on the fire. "Guess that's what happens when your Pa raises you as a boy."

Nash tilted his head, intrigued. "What do you mean by that?"

She leaned back, resting her hands behind her, and looked at him squarely. "Exactly what I said. Ma died when I was born. Pa already had two boys, and when I came along, he didn't know what to do with a girl. So he decided not to bother tryin'. Said he knew how to raise boys and figured I'd just have to fit in."

There was no bitterness in her tone, only the steady cadence of someone recounting facts. "So, I learned to ride, rope, shoot, and spit just like my brothers. We worked cattle together, broke horses, hunted game. Pa didn't give me any slack 'cause I was smaller. Said if I couldn't keep up, I'd be left behind."

Nash studied her for a moment, the flickering firelight playing across her sharp features. "Didn't bother you?"

"Why would it?" she shot back with a shrug. "It was just the way things were. Ain't like I knew anything different. Besides," she added, a sly grin tugging at her lips, "I liked being out there, doing what they did. Never cared much for the idea of being stuck inside with needlework or baking pies."

"Fair enough," Nash said, nodding. He leaned forward, his forearms resting on his knees. "Where are they now? Your Pa and your brothers?"

The grin slipped from Willa's face, her expression turning distant. She shrugged, poking the fire again with her stick. "Dead, I guess. They went off to fight in the war and never came back. Pa left me to look after the ranch, but it didn't take long before the banks came sniffing around. Lost the land before I even had a chance to fight for it."

She tossed the stick into the fire and dusted her hands off on her trousers, her movements brisk, almost dismissive. "That's life, though, ain't it? Nothing sticks around forever."

Nash didn't respond immediately. He studied her face, the way she kept her gaze on the fire as if daring him to offer pity. He could see the resilience in her, the way her jaw tightened just slightly when she mentioned the ranch or her family.

"Hell of a thing," Nash said finally, his voice quiet. "You've been through it."

"Everyone's been through it," Willa replied, meeting his eyes with a sharp look. "Ain't no use crying over what's gone. You either keep moving, or you let it bury you. Me? I keep moving."

Nash gave a faint smile and nodded, tipping his hat back slightly. "That you do, Willa. That you do."

For a moment, they sat in silence, the crackle of the fire filling the space between them. Nash couldn't help but feel a flicker of admiration for her, even if he knew better than to say so. Willa wasn't the type to take kindly to compliments, and he wasn't the type to hand them out lightly.

Willa leaned back against a boulder, her sharp gaze fixed on Nash as she twirled a blade of grass between her fingers. She had that look about her all of a sudden, one he recognised—the kind that said she was gearing up to pry something loose. Nash wasn't sure he liked it.

"So, what's your story, cowboy?" she asked, her tone casual but edged with curiosity. "And don't give me that 'just passing through' line. I've been around enough to know there's always more to it."

Nash adjusted his hat, the brim shadowing his eyes. "Not much to tell," he muttered, poking at the ground with a stick.

Willa snorted, unconvinced. "Sure. A man like you doesn't end up as good with a gun as you are without a reason. You've got the look of someone who's been running from something—or chasing it. Which is it?"

Nash shot her a sharp glance but didn't respond. Willa wasn't deterred.

"And another thing," she said, her tone thoughtful now. "I'd bet money you've got Indian blood in you. Cherokee?

Comanche? You've got that bone structure, the eyes." She tilted her head, studying him like he was a puzzle she intended to solve.

Nash stiffened, his fingers tightening around the stick. "You ask a lot of questions," he said evenly.

"Only when I want answers," Willa shot back, a slight smirk playing on her lips.

For a moment, Nash was silent, the flicker of the firelight casting shadows across his face. When he finally spoke, his voice was quieter, more hesitant than Willa had expected.

"My ma was Apache," he said, his words measured like he was testing how much he wanted to say. "My pa was Irish. Came over from Kerry to work the mines. They met in Georgia, back when things were... different."

"Different, how?" Willa asked, her voice softer now.

Nash shrugged, staring into the fire as if it held the answers. "Different as in not good. My pa's people didn't take kindly to him marrying an Indian woman. And Ma's family... well, they didn't trust white folks much either. We lived on the edges of things, always moving."

Willa watched him closely, sensing the weight behind the few words he offered. "That's why you're still moving?" she asked gently.

Nash chuckled dryly, shaking his head. "Maybe. Or maybe it's just the only thing I've ever been good at."

Willa didn't press him further, sensing his reluctance. Instead, she leaned back again, her gaze still on him but less probing now. "Well," she said after a long pause, "you've got the look of someone who's seen a lot more than he lets on. But don't worry, I ain't about to pry it all out of you. Yet."

Nash glanced at her, a faint smile tugging at the corner of his mouth. "Mighty kind of you."

"Don't mention it," Willa replied with a smirk. But her tone softened as she added, "Just don't expect me to spill my guts if you're holding yours back."

Nash chuckled again, low and quiet. "Fair enough."

The conversation ebbed, the silence between them settling into something almost comfortable. Nash shifted his hat lower over his eyes, grateful that Willa didn't push further. Some things, he reckoned, were better left unsaid—for now. The fire crackled between them, sending sparks into the cool night air. Willa shifted her position slightly, tossing another piece of wood into the flames. She was quiet for a while, her sharp gaze studying Nash in that way she had as if she could read the man better than he wanted.

"You're good with that iron," she said finally, her tone as casual as if she were commenting on the weather. "Real good. Too good for it to be just instinct. Who taught you?"

Nash's jaw tightened, his eyes fixed on the flames. The flickering light cast shadows over his face, deepening the hard lines there. He didn't answer immediately, and Willa leaned forward slightly, sensing something heavy in his silence.

"Come on," she pressed, her voice edging toward curiosity. "A man doesn't get as quick and as deadly as you are without a teacher. Who was it?"

For a long moment, Nash didn't move. When he finally spoke, his voice was low, almost reluctant. "A man I rode with once," he said, the words clipped.

"Who?" Willa asked, sitting up straighter now.

Nash exhaled through his nose, his grip tightening on the brim of his hat. "Cain," he said, at last, the name coming out like a confession. "Luke Cain."

The name hung in the air, heavy and sharp as a knife. Willa's expression shifted in an instant. Her easy camaraderie vanished, replaced by something colder—mistrust, suspicion. She leaned back slightly, her hand resting near the butt of her revolver.

"Luke Cain," she repeated, her voice flat. "I know that name. Hard not to, if you've spent any time around a sheriff's office. He had his face on a few posters, didn't he? Wanted for robbery, murder, and just about every sin under the sun."

Nash looked up, meeting her eyes for the first time since the name had left his lips. The flicker of firelight in his gaze was darker now, weighted with something that made Willa's fingers twitch near her gun.

"Yeah," he said evenly. "He had his face on a few posters."

"And you rode with him," Willa said, her tone sharpening. "You're telling me you rode with Luke Cain, a man half the lawmen of the west were chasing?"

Nash didn't flinch under her scrutiny, but his jaw tightened further. "I rode with him. A while ago."

Willa's lips pressed into a thin line, her eyes narrowing. "And here I was, thinking you might be one of the good ones. Guess I should've known better."

Nash let the comment hang for a moment before responding, his tone low but firm. "You think I'm proud of it? You think I don't regret every damned day I spent in his shadow?"

Willa's hand eased slightly, but her expression stayed hard. "Why'd you do it, then? Ride with a man like that?"

Nash's eyes drifted back to the fire, the flickering flames reflecting in his gaze like ghosts of another time. "Because back then, I didn't know any better. I thought Cain had all the answers; I thought he was untouchable. He wasn't just quick with a gun—he was smart and ruthless. The kind of man who could make you believe he was invincible. And when I met him, I didn't know what he'd done either. I rescued him from a group of Comanche who were about to beat him to death."

"And you?" Willa asked, her voice quieter now. "What'd he make you believe about yourself?"

Nash hesitated, his fingers tightening on the brim of his hat. "That I didn't have a choice."

The words hung between them, heavy and raw. Willa studied him for a long moment, the suspicion in her eyes tempered now by something softer—understanding, maybe, or at least a willingness to listen.

Finally, she leaned back, her hand moving away from her revolver. "Well," she said, her tone still cautious, "I guess even the best of us make mistakes."

Nash glanced up at her, his expression unreadable.

"Don't think I won't keep my eye on you, cowboy. I've got no love for men who make the wrong kind of choices." Willa said, a hint of a smirk tugging at the corner of her mouth.

"Fair enough," Nash replied, tipping his hat slightly. But as the conversation drifted into silence.

Nash sat cross-legged on the ground, his back against a boulder, the weight of the day settling over him like an old, unwanted coat. The stars above seemed indifferent, their cold light piercing through the darkness of the wilderness. Nash tugged his hat low over his eyes, but he didn't sleep. Not yet.

His mind wandered back, unwillingly, to a time he'd tried to bury—Luke Cain's last moments.

He could still see the gallows clearly, the rough-hewn wood rising starkly against the dusty horizon. The crowd had gathered early that day, their voices a mix of righteous anger and morbid curiosity. Nash had been mounted on his mare at the back of the crowd, about to ride out of town.

Cain stood on the platform, his hands bound, his head held high. The noose dangled at his side, a silent predator waiting to claim him. But Cain wasn't afraid. Not Luke Cain. If anything, he looked amused, as if the entire affair was nothing more than a cruel joke played on everyone but him. That expression had burned itself into Nash's memory—smug, mocking, and full of contempt.

"Any last words?" the hangman had asked, his voice a monotone formality.

Cain's lips had curled into that damned smirk, the one that had always made Nash's blood boil. He scanned the crowd, his sharp eyes finding Nash almost immediately like he'd known exactly where he'd be. Nash had frozen, his heart hammering in his chest as Cain's gaze locked onto him.

"You're just like me," Cain had mouthed the words.

Cain dropped. The rope snapped taut with a sickening finality, and just like that, it was over. But the look on Cain's face—smug, almost triumphant—lingered in Nash's mind long after his body had gone still.

Now, by the firelight, Nash clenched his jaw, trying to shake the memory loose. He stared into the flames, his hand absently tracing the worn grip of his Colt. He'd spent years trying to prove Cain wrong, to prove to himself that he wasn't just another shadow cast by the man who had once towered over him.

But in moments like this, when the night was quiet and the ghosts crept in, doubt gnawed at him. Cain had been a liar, a thief, and a killer, but he'd also been a man who knew how to read people—knew how to get under their skin. And Nash couldn't ignore the bitter truth: some days, he saw more of Luke Cain in himself than he cared to admit.

The fire popped, sending a spray of embers into the air, and Nash flinched and pulled back to the present. He leaned forward, resting his elbows on his knees, his eyes dark and distant. He didn't sleep well that night. He never did, not when Cain's words echoed so loudly in the quiet.

As the flames flickered lower, Nash finally stretched out on his bedroll, his Colt close at hand. He closed his eyes, but rest eluded him, chased away by the shadow of a man who refused to stay buried.

CHAPTER SEVEN

The trail ahead was quiet, the morning stillness broken only by the rhythmic clop of hooves and the occasional rustle of leaves in the gentle breeze. Nash and Willa had been riding in silence, both lost in thought, the weight of their shared purpose pressing heavily on their shoulders.

As they rounded a bend in the trail, Nash's mare snorted and tossed her head, the faint metallic tang of blood carried on the breeze. He held up a hand, signaling Willa to stop. She reined in her horse, her sharp eyes scanning the underbrush.

"What is it?" she asked, her voice low.

Nash slid from the saddle, his boots crunching softly against the dirt as he moved forward. "Blood trail," he muttered, nodding toward the splatters staining the dusty path. The droplets grew darker and thicker as they followed the trail into the trees. He motioned for Willa to cover him as he moved cautiously ahead.

Just beyond a cluster of pines, Nash spotted a figure slumped against the trunk of a tree. The man's chest rose and fell in labored breaths, his shirt soaked with blood from a ragged wound on his arm. His horse stood a few feet away, reins tangled in the underbrush, its sides heaving as if it had been running hard before its rider had fallen.

Nash crouched beside the wounded man, his eyes sharp and calculating as he took in the outlaw's pale face and the sweat glistening on his forehead. The wound on his arm was deep, a ragged tear of flesh that was oozing thick, dark blood. The man's breathing was shallow, each inhale rattling in his chest, and Nash could tell he wouldn't last long without help.

He glanced up at Willa, who was standing with one foot propped on a rock, her rifle resting easily against her shoulder. She was watching the outlaw with a detached, almost bored expression, but Nash didn't miss the way her fingers curled just a little tighter around the rifle's grip.

"You're lucky, Willa only winged you," Nash drawled, tipping his hat back slightly. "I got half a mind to leave you to the coyotes, but I'm feelin' charitable today."

The outlaw's lips curled into a weak sneer. "Charitable? You ain't got a charitable bone in your body, mister."

Willa snorted softly, drawing Nash's attention. "You sure you got this one pegged as mine?" she asked, arching a brow. "I don't do 'winging,' Nash. If he's breathing, it ain't because of me."

Nash chuckled, the sound low and amused. "Well, I hate to break it to you, but unless this fella here shot himself, I'd say you were off your mark for once." He gestured to the wound. "Looks like you might've just grazed him, after all."

Willa's eyes narrowed, her mouth tugging into something that wasn't quite a smile. "Maybe I was feelin' charitable too."

Nash grinned at that, shaking his head as he turned his attention back to the wounded man. "Alright, friend, here's how this works. You start talkin', and we'll see about keepin' you from leaking all over the ground. Otherwise, you can enjoy a long, slow death." He pulled a bandana from his pocket and dangled it in front of the outlaw. "Your call."

The outlaw's chest heaved as he struggled to sit up straighter, wincing in pain. His eyes darted to Willa, lingering on her rifle, then back to Nash. "I ain't got nothin' to say."

"Suit yourself." Nash tucked the bandana back into his pocket and started to rise. "And we'll be helping ourselves to your horse and anything else we take a fancy to."

"Wait." The word came out rough, choked with pain. "I ain't... I ain't part of them no more. I can't go back to Slade's outfit now."

Willa crouched down beside Nash, her sharp gaze drilling into the outlaw. "That's what happens when you're dead weight. What happened back there?"

The man swallowed hard, his gaze flicking between them. "Slade knew you were on our tail, left four of us to deal with you... he doesn't like loose ends. Took a bullet from one of you, and if I go back to Slade now, he'll put another in me for not stopping you." He coughed, a harsh, rattling sound that made Nash's gut tighten.

Nash nodded slowly. "Where'd they head?"

The outlaw hesitated, licking his dry lips. "South," he rasped. "Toward the dry washes, there's a canyon he uses as a camp. The entrance between the rocks is hard to see, and it's narrow. There's a horseshoe ridge and a mark in the rocks looks like a crescent, and it's to the left of that."

Nash's eyes were steady and unyielding. "How many men does Slade have?"

The outlaw shifted uncomfortably, his face pale and slick with sweat. He hesitated, his brow furrowing as if counting wasn't exactly his strong suit.

"Well..." he drawled, buying himself a moment. "More'n a few."

Nash's patience thinned. "You know how many are in a dozen, don't you?" His voice was flat, unimpressed.

The outlaw swallowed hard and nodded quickly. "Yeah... yeah, I know."

"Good," Nash said, his gaze pinning the man in place. "So how many dozens we talkin'?"

The outlaw glanced away, his lips moving slightly as if doing the math in his head. Finally, he sighed. "Three, I reckon. Maybe a couple more if Slade's been recruitin'."

Nash exchanged a glance with Willa, who arched an eyebrow, unimpressed. "Three dozen," Nash repeated, his tone dry. "You could've just said thirty-six."

The outlaw managed a weak grin. "I ain't much for figurin', mister."

Nash gave a slow nod, standing up and dusting off his hands. "Yeah, I'm startin' to see that."

Willa looked at Nash, her expression thoughtful. "Could be truth, could be a pile of horseshit."

Nash considered the outlaw for a long moment, his gaze unreadable. "We'll find out soon enough." He reached for the bandana again, pressing it against the man's wound with a little more force than necessary, earning a grunt of pain. "Might be your lucky day after all."

Willa stood, dusting off her hands. "His luck day was yesterday when your aim was off," she quipped, and for the first time in days, Nash allowed himself a small, genuine smile.

Nash shot Willa a sidelong glance. "Guess I'll have to start keepin' score."

She smirked. "You couldn't keep up."

When Nash finished, he stepped back and wiped his hands on his pants. "He'll live," he said, his tone flat. Nash then fixed the man with a cold stare. "You stay put until morning, you hear? Try to follow us, and I'll make sure you don't get a second chance."

The outlaw nodded, his defiance extinguished.

As the light faded, Nash and Willa set up camp a safe distance from where they'd left the outlaw. The fire crackled softly, casting flickering shadows across their faces as they poured over the information they'd gathered.

"A horseshoe ridge," Willa said, tracing a map with her finger. "There's only one place that matches that description south of here."

"Means he wasn't lyin'," Nash said, his gaze distant. He leaned back against a tree. "But if Slade has that many men, we can't just walk in guns blazing."

Willa smirked. "Wasn't plannin' on it. What're you thinkin'?"

"First, we scout the place," Nash said. "See how many men he's got, where they're positioned, and what kind of setup we're dealin' with. Runnin' in blind'll just get us killed. We've already trimmed down his numbers, so that's good, but he's gonna know about that soon enough, and it'll make him edgy."

Willa nodded, her expression thoughtful. "And once we've got the lay of the land?"

Nash's lips pressed into a thin line. "We'll figure that out when we get there. One step at a time."

The firelight danced in Willa's eyes as she studied him. "You're a careful man," she said. "I can respect that. But careful only gets you so far."

"Careful's kept me alive this long," Nash replied, his tone quiet but firm.

They fell into a comfortable silence, the night wrapping around them like a heavy blanket. Nash stared into the fire, his mind already racing ahead to what awaited them in the canyon. He didn't trust Slade's men to play fair, but he'd learned long ago that fairness didn't matter. What mattered was being one step ahead.

And this time, he intended to stay there.

The next morning, Nash and Willa rode south, the early light casting long shadows across the rugged terrain. The forest gave way to rolling hills, and soon, they spotted the ridge the outlaw had described—a natural formation that curved into a horseshoe, its jagged edges rising like the teeth of some ancient beast.

They dismounted a safe distance away, tying their horses to a cluster of scrub trees. Willa pulled out a spyglass, extending it with a practiced motion as she crouched behind a boulder.

"See anything?" Nash asked, crouching beside her.

"Yeah, there's a rockfall; it's shaped like a crescent. Seems he was tellin' the truth. And there's guards up on the ridge," Willa said, her voice low. She passed the spyglass to him, pointing toward the ridge. "There, on the east side. And another pair by the entrance."

Nash studied the scene for a moment, then lowered the glass. "They're not amateurs," he said. "Positions are good—hard to approach without bein' seen. Means we'll have to get creative," Nash said, his tone grim. He leaned back, folding the spyglass and handing it back. "First step's findin' a way in without raisin' the alarm."

Willa grinned, her eyes glinting with mischief. "Good thing I'm creative."

Nash shook his head, a faint smirk tugging at his lips. "Let's just hope that your creativity doesn't get us killed."

Willa glanced up at the winding ridge stretching out before them, her expression turning thoughtful. "We could keep moving along the ridge," she suggested, pointing with her arm. "Then circle back, either along the top or down at the base."

Nash considered the idea, his eyes narrowing as he scanned the terrain ahead. "The top might be better," he said after a beat. "Give us a good view of the camp, see what we're walking into. But it depends on how much cover we've got up there."

Willa nodded, weighing the options. "Yeah. If it's too exposed, we'll have to take the low ground." She shifted her stance, rubbing her thumb over the stock of her rifle. "Either way, we'll leave the horses here. Go in on foot."

Nash glanced back at their mounts, the animals standing quietly, hobbled in the brush. "Agreed. Last thing we need is a spooked horse givin' us away."

They both turned their eyes to the ridge again, the wind stirring the dry grass around them. The sun was sinking lower, casting long shadows over the landscape.

"We'd best get movin'," Willa said. "We'll figure the rest once we're closer."

Nash gave her a curt nod. "Let's go."

They moved carefully along the edge of the ridge, their boots crunching softly against the rocky earth. Nash led the way, his eyes sharp, constantly scanning for any sign of movement below. Willa followed, her steps light and sure, her rifle held ready in case trouble found them sooner than expected.

After a while, Nash slowed, crouching behind a cluster of boulders and gesturing for Willa to do the same. He peered ahead, studying the terrain with a practiced eye. "If we take the high ground," he murmured, "we'll have a good angle, but we'll need to keep low. If Slade's got a lookout posted, we could get spotted real quick."

Willa shrugged, her voice steady. "Risky either way. But up top, we can see them before they see us. Down low, we're blind until we're right on top of 'em."

Nash exhaled through his nose, thinking it over. "Alright. We'll head up, take it slow, and keep close to the rocks." He met her gaze. "If things go south, we pull back and regroup at the horses."

"Sounds fair," Willa agreed, her lips twitching into a wry smile. "I like a man with a plan."

Nash gave her a look deadpan. "I like a plan that keeps me alive."

Willa chuckled under her breath. "Come on, cowboy. Let's see what's waitin' for us up there."

With one last glance at the camp far below, they moved carefully along the ridge, shadows stretching ahead of them as the sun dipped closer to the horizon.

CHAPTER EIGHT

Nash and Willa moved slowly along the top of the ridge. As they moved, they were careful to keep their silhouettes low against the backdrop of the rocky skyline. The sun, hanging low on the horizon, bathed the landscape in an amber glow, stretching its shadows long across the cracked earth. Every step was deliberate, their boots crunching lightly on loose gravel, the only sound other than the occasional whisper of wind through the dry scrub.

Nash led the way, his sharp eyes scanning the terrain ahead. The ridge was rugged, littered with jagged outcroppings and scattered boulders that provided some cover but not nearly enough for his liking. Nash paused with every few steps, crouching low behind a rock or bush, listening and watching for any sign of movement below. The gang's sentries were out there somewhere, and one careless step could give them away.

Behind him, Willa moved with practiced ease, her steps light, rifle cradled across her chest. Her breathing was steady, but Nash didn't miss the way her gaze swept the canyon below with the same wary sharpness he carried. She wasn't just a bounty hunter—she was a survivor, and he respected that.

They came to a narrow section of the ridge, the trail pinching tight between a lethal sheer drop on one side and on the other a towering rock face. Nash paused, placing a hand flat against the cool stone, listening. He could hear the distant murmur of voices from the canyon below— too far to make out words, but close enough to remind him just how dangerous their position was.

Willa pressed in close behind him, her voice barely above a whisper. "You see anythin'?"

"Not yet," Nash murmured back, his eyes flicking to a rocky outcrop further along the ridge where the land flattened out. "There's a good vantage point up ahead. If we can get to it without bein' seen, we'll have eyes on the whole camp."

Willa nodded, adjusting her stance. "Let's hope your luck holds."

Nash smirked faintly. "Ain't much on luck. Just patience."

With that, he moved forward again, careful to stay low as they crept along the narrow pass. Loose stones crumbled under his boots, tumbling noisily down the slope. He froze, muscles tensing as he glanced down toward the canyon, watching for any sign that they'd been noticed. Below, a figure moved near the campfire, pausing briefly to glance in their direction. Nash held his breath, watching as the outlaw seemed to consider something before turning back to his companions.

Nash let out a slow breath and pressed on, keeping to the deeper shadows where the fading sunlight couldn't reach. As they neared the outcrop, a sudden sound made them both freeze—a faint rustling from the ridge below. Nash instinctively raised a hand, signaling Willa to hold back. He pressed himself against the rock, feeling the sharp angles press into his back, peering carefully over the edge.

There was a lone sentry standing below them; he was leaning lazily against a boulder with his rifle resting on his lap. His hat was pulled low, and he sipped from a tin cup, oblivious to the danger lurking just above him. Nash studied him for a moment, considering their options.

Willa edged up beside him, her voice barely above a whisper, her head close to his. "We takin' him out?"
Nash shook his head. "Not yet. If he doesn't see us, no need to stir up a hornet's nest."

They inched forward again, finally reaching the outcrop Nash had spotted earlier. From here, the entire canyon spread out before them, revealing the gang's hideout nestled deep within the rock formations. Smoke curled lazily from the central fire, figures moving around in the fading light. Makeshift lean-tos and shacks clustered tightly together, and Nash counted at least a dozen men moving about—probably more inside the structures.

The sun was sinking fast now, casting long shadows that stretched across the canyon floor. Nash lowered himself onto his stomach, resting his forearms against the warm rock, Willa pulled the spyglass from her coat and handed it to Nash first, nodding toward the camp.

"Take a look. Get a feel for the place."

He took it without a word, scanning the camp with a keen eye. The gang's hideout sprawled across the canyon floor like a scorpion's nest, a haphazard collection of rough-hewn shacks, lean-tos, and canvas tents pitched against the jagged rock walls. A winding dirt path snaked through the camp, trampled and well-worn from constant use, leading to a larger central structure that looked sturdier than the rest—probably Slade's quarters.

A large fire was burning in the middle of the camp, its flickering light casting long shadows against the rock walls and sending a spire of smoke up over. Around it, several men sat hunched on crates and makeshift benches, nursing tin cups and laughing in low, rough voices. One of them, a heavyset man with a thick beard and a battered hat, poked at the fire with a stick, his actions sending embers spiraling into the night air, drifting up over with the smoke. The smell of roasting meat drifted up the canyon, mingling with the acrid scent of gun oil and unwashed bodies and horse muck.

To the left of the fire, a pair of outlaws were huddled around a small table, playing cards under the dim glow of a lantern. Their faces were hard and weathered, their eyes darting nervously toward their surroundings with the wary tension of men who lived by the gun. A pile of coins and a bottle of whiskey sat between them, but the way one of them kept his hand close to his revolver spoke to the kind of stakes they were playing for.

Further back, near a rusted water trough, a younger kid with a wiry frame was tending to a string of horses, brushing down their coats and checking their tack with the efficiency of someone who had done it a thousand times before.

Near the rock face, a lean man in a long duster coat stood with his arms crossed, watching the camp with the cold detachment of someone who held authority. Nash guessed he was one of Slade's lieutenants if not Slade himself. Behind him, a few more outlaws were unloading supplies from a wagon—crates of ammunition and sacks that could've held anything from food to stolen gold.

To the far right of the camp, a group of men gathered around what looked like a makeshift blacksmith's station. A burly man with soot-streaked hands worked a bellows, the glow of hot iron reflecting off his sweat-slicked brow. The rhythmic clang of a hammer against metal echoed through the canyon, covering the occasional bursts of drunken laughter from the men around the fire.

Nash's eyes lingered on a shadowy area near the mouth of the canyon, where a pair of guards stood watch, rifles resting lazily in their hands. They looked bored, one of them leaning against a boulder while the other chewed on a piece of jerky, but Nash knew better than to underestimate them. The trail leading in and out of the hideout was narrow and steep.

Nash handed it back, his lips pressing into a thin line. "They're not amateurs," he said. "Positions are good—hard to approach without bein' seen, and there's a lot more of them than I'd hoped."

"They're spread out," Willa muttered, her voice barely above a whisper. "Sloppy, but they've got the high ground locked down."

Nash nodded. "That ridge on the south side has a clear view of the canyon floor. Any fool tryin' to charge it would be picked off before they got halfway."

"You've done this before," Willa remarked, glancing at him with a small smirk.

Nash didn't reply immediately. His eyes followed the movements of two sentries pacing along the ridge, their rifles slung casually over their shoulders. One of them stopped to spit over the edge, his demeanor lazy. The other leaned against a boulder, gazing off into the distance.

"They ain't expectin' trouble," Nash said finally. "Makes 'em careless."

"Careless is good," Willa said, tapping her fingers lightly against the stock of her rifle. "Gives us an edge."

The two spent the better part of an hour observing the camp. Nash noted the positions of the sentries, the paths they patrolled, and the routines of the men below. A corral of tired-looking horses was situated near the entrance to the canyon, guarded by two more men.

As Nash and Willa retraced their steps along the ridge, the fading light painted the landscape in hues of deep amber and dusky purple. The canyon below was quiet now, the campfires flickering like distant stars against the darkening ground. They moved in silence, each footstep carefully placed to avoid the loose gravel that could betray their presence.

Nash's mind worked as they moved, thoughts churning like the restless wind that whispered through the scrub. There were too many of them—too many guns, too many eyes watching the camp. It was clear now that taking down Slade's gang wouldn't be a simple job, not with just the two of them. He glanced at Willa ahead of him, her silhouette sharp against the ridgeline, moving with the ease of someone who knew how to stay in the shadows.

As they returned to the spot where they had left their horses, Nash's thoughts were already turning to their next move. They needed more firepower, more hands. They couldn't do this alone. A full-on assault would be suicide with just the two of them, but if they could pick them apart, find weaknesses, sow a little fear—maybe, just maybe, they'd stand a chance. The idea gnawed at him, practical yet dangerous. He'd fought gangs before; the Red Vultures had to be dismantled from the inside; he'd never been able to take them down another way. For that, though, there just wasn't the time.

They reached the small cluster of boulders where their horses were hobbled, hidden among the sparse brush. Nash crouched beside his mare, running a hand over her flank to soothe her as she shifted anxiously. He glanced at Willa, who was checking the straps on her saddle, her face set in a thoughtful frown.

"We're outnumbered," he finally muttered, keeping his voice low. "Just us two ain't gonna cut it."

Willa didn't look up, but he saw the slight nod of her head. "I was thinkin' the same thing. We need help."

CHAPTER NINE

The campfire was casting flickering shadows across the clearing, its light dancing on Willa's determined face, highlighting her fine features and narrow face. Nash sat on a log; he was rolling a twig between his fingers, his brow furrowed in thought. Willa leaned against her saddle, arms crossed, her sharp gaze fixed on him.

"We can't do this alone," Willa said, her voice cutting through the quiet. "You know that, right?"

Nash glanced up at her, his eyes narrowing. "I don't like involving others in my business."

"This isn't just your business," she shot back, pushing off the saddle to stand. "Slade's gang isn't just robbing banks—they're leaving a trail of bodies. If you want to clear your name and stop them for good, you're gonna need more firepower than what we've got."

Nash tossed the twig into the fire, watching it crackle and blacken. "You think the sheriff's gonna listen to a wanted man?"

"That's why *I'm* going," Willa said. "The Sheriff knows me, and more importantly, he knows my reputation. He might not like me, but he'll take me seriously."

Nash let out a low sigh, rubbing the back of his neck. "And what's your plan, exactly? Waltz into town and convince him to go up against Slade's gang with a handful of deputies?"

Willa's expression hardened. "You've got a better idea? Look, the Sheriff may be in over his head, but he's got a badge, and that badge means something to the people in Ironwood. We don't need an army, Nash—just enough men who can shoot straight and hold their ground."

"And if the sheriff decides he'd rather lock me up than help?" Nash asked, his tone skeptical.

"Then you stay here and let me handle it," Willa said. "But I'm not letting Slade keep running wild while you brood about trust."

Nash studied her for a long moment, his jaw tight. He didn't like relying on others—it wasn't in his nature. But she was right. There were too many outlaws, and they couldn't take them on alone.

Finally, he nodded, his voice low and reluctant. "Alright. You go talk to the Sheriff. I'll wait here."

Willa smirked, though there was no humor in it. "Glad you're finally seeing reason."

Nash leaned back, crossing his arms. "Just don't get yourself killed, Callahan."

She raised an eyebrow, a glimmer of amusement in her dark eyes. "Don't you worry about me, cowboy? I've been doing this for a long time. I'll head off at first light."

Nash watched Willa for a moment with a mix of admiration and unease. He didn't trust easily, but if anyone could pull this off, it was her. Still, he couldn't shake the feeling that their fight was only just beginning.

In the morning, the sky had turned a dull gray, clouds threatening rain as Willa and Nash crouched near a cluster of trees, surveying the dusty trail that led back into Ironwood. Nash sat cross-legged, his Colt resting on his thigh, while Willa tightened the straps on her saddle.

"You still sure about this?" Nash asked, his voice low and gravelly. His eyes stayed fixed on the town in the distance, a flicker of concern crossing his face.

"I'm not the one they want to hang," Willa replied, her tone dry as she adjusted her wide-brimmed hat. "Let me handle it."

Nash frowned. "The Sheriff's a cautious man, but he's not blind. He'll listen if you lay it out clearly."

"Maybe." She mounted her horse in one smooth motion. "But I'm not doin' this for free. There's a bounty on Slade's head, and if I'm risking my neck for this town, I'm damn sure gonna get my cut."

Nash smirked despite himself. "Didn't take you for the money-hungry type."

"It's not hunger, cowboy. It's survival," Willa shot back, giving him a sharp look. "You keep your head down and stay out of sight. If this goes south, I'll be back for you. Maybe."

With that, she urged her horse forward, leaving Nash in the shadow of the trees. He watched her ride off, the sway of her hat and the determined set of her shoulders catching his attention in a way he wasn't expecting. He shook his head, muttering to himself, *This is business. Don't complicate it.*

Willa rode into Ironwood as the sun rose, casting long shadows across the street. The town was subdued, the air thick with unease after the recent violence. She pulled up in front of the Sheriff's office, tying her horse to the hitching post with deliberate care. Her rifle hung from her shoulder, and her hand hovered near the revolver on her hip.

Sheriff Anders looked up from his desk when Willa strode through the door.

His expression was a mix of weariness and suspicion, the lines on his face deepening as he leaned back in his chair, regarding her with a narrowed gaze. To his left was a deputy, his eyes running over Willas as she stepped into the office, missing nothing; his mouth twitched into an amused smile.

"Callahan," Anders greeted, his tone wary. "What brings you here?"

"Trouble," Willa replied bluntly, shutting the door behind her. "You've got a bigger problem than you realize, Sheriff." Anders raised an eyebrow. "If this is about the raid on the bank?"

"It is," Willa interrupted, stepping closer. "That gang you've been chasing? Slade's boys? They're the real culprits behind the bank robbery, and I know where they're holed up. That drifter had nothing to do with it."

The Sheriff leaned forward, his elbows resting on the desk. "You've got proof of that?"

Willa's lips tightened. "Not yet. But we've tracked them to a canyon north of here. They've got a hideout and enough firepower to burn this town to the ground."

Sheriff Anders leaned back in his chair, his hand idly brushing the handle of his revolver as his sharp eyes studied Willa. "Miss Callahan, I've got half the town ready to lynch that drifter you're defendin'. The Elders are a powerful family, and they've put a bounty on his head. If you think I'm about to side with a man wanted for killin' Dan Elder, you're sorely mistaken."

Willa's jaw tightened. She took a measured step closer to the desk, her rifle still slung across her shoulder but her presence unmistakably commanding. "You think this is about some damned drifter? I'm tellin' you, Sheriff, the real threat is Slade and his men. If you keep chasin' the wrong man, this town's gonna be ashes before you've got the chance to say 'I told you so.'"

Anders scoffed, leaning forward. "You expect me to just take your word for it? That drifter's got blood on his hands, and the town won't rest easy till he's brought to justice."

"Justice?" Willa snapped. "Is that what you call this? Chasin' the wrong man while the real killers are holed up with enough firepower to level Ironwood? You've got two choices here, Sheriff. You trust me, or you dig this town's grave with your own stubborn pride."

Anders frowned, his fingers tapping a slow rhythm on the desk. "And what's your angle in all this, Callahan? A woman like you doesn't ride into a mess like this without somethin' to gain."

Willa smirked, though there was no humor in it. "Slade's got a bounty on his head—a big one. All I want is my share of the money, and I'll take you right to his hideout."

Anders mulled that over, his brow furrowed in thought. "And what about the drifter? You expect me to let him ride off scot-free?"

Willa crossed her arms, her stance firm. "Nash is the reason I even know where Slade's gang is hidin'. He's been trackin' them just like I have."

Anders was silent for a long moment, the weight of his position pressing down on him. Finally, he sighed, scrubbing a hand over his face. "Alright, Callahan. I'll play along—for now. But if Nash shows up, he's coming right back here to a cell, you hear me, and the law can decide if he's innocent or not."

Willa nodded, her expression unreadable. "Fair enough."

Anders pointed a finger at her as she turned to leave. "Remember, Callahan, this ain't no free ride. If this goes wrong, the town'll put the blame on both of us."

Willa paused at the door, her hand on the frame. "Don't worry, Sheriff. It won't—because I'm not gonna let it."

Willa turned on her heel, the Sheriff's ultimatum still fresh in her ears. Her mind was already on the trail ahead, but the low whistle of one of Anders' deputies cut through her focus. She froze mid-step as the man stepped into her path, a smirk plastered across his face.

The deputy was tall, broad-shouldered, with the kind of swagger that spoke of too much confidence and too little reason to back it up. He leaned toward her slightly, his hand darting out with a casual, lewd audacity. His fingers squeezed her rear, the sound of his laughter grating in the already-tense room, and his breath foul against her cheek.

"I just wanted to know," he said, his voice dripping with mockery, "if you're as hard on the inside as you make out."

Willa stopped dead, her body stiffening. For a second, the room seemed to hold its breath. Then, in one fluid motion, her rifle swung up, the butt of it driving hard into the underside of the deputy's chin.

The crack of impact was sharp and brutal, sending the man staggering backward. His hat flew off, and he crumpled against the wall, one hand clutching his bleeding mouth while the other flailed to steady himself. A streak of crimson leaked through his fingers, his cocky grin now replaced by a look of stunned pain.

"There's your answer," Willa said flatly, her voice as cold and sharp as the blow she'd just delivered.

Sheriff Anders, who had been watching the exchange from behind his desk, didn't move at first. His lips tightened, and then he let out a sigh, shaking his head as he fixed his deputy with a hard glare.

"You damn well asked for that," Anders said, his tone carrying no sympathy. "What the hell were you thinkin', Charlie?"

Charlie tried to sputter out a response, but the blood filling his mouth made it unintelligible. He slumped into a chair, glaring at Willa with watery, reddened eyes.

Willa leveled her gaze at him, her hands steady on the rifle. "You put your hands on me again, you'll be needin' more than a rag to stop the bleeding."

Anders leaned back in his chair, the tension in the room thick enough to cut. He waved a dismissive hand at the whimpering deputy. "Get yourself cleaned up, Charlie. And next time, keep your damn hands to yourself."

Willa turned without another word, pushing the door open with enough force to make it rattle on its hinges. Out in the street, she tugged her hat down against the sun, mounting her horse with a practiced ease.

Inside the office, Anders stared at the bloodied deputy for a long moment before shaking his head again. "Idiot," he muttered, grabbing his rifle and following Willa out.

Sheriff Anders and his small party rode out from Ironwood as the sun climbed higher, the land stretching wide and open before them. Willa rode a few paces behind the Sheriff, her rifle strapped to her saddle and her hat pulled low against the glare. The deputies followed close behind, including Charlie, whose bruised jaw and surly scowl were a testament to his earlier altercation with her. Willa caught the occasional malevolent glance he shot her way, but she ignored him, focusing on the trail ahead.

The Eldon Ranch came into view as they crested a low hill. It was a sprawling operation, the kind that spoke of wealth and hard work. The main house stood tall and proud, with a large barn and several outbuildings spread out around it. Smoke drifted from the chimney, and a couple of ranch hands paused in their work to eye the approaching riders, tools held still in their hands, and suspicion in their eyes.

Dan Eldon's widow, Martha, stood on the porch as they arrived, her black dress a stark reminder of her recent mourning. Her sons, Casey and Tom, flanked her, both broad-shouldered and grim-faced, their resemblance to their late father unmistakable.

Sheriff Anders dismounted, dusting off his hat as he approached the porch. "Mrs. Eldon, Casey, Tom," he greeted with a respectful nod. "I appreciate you taking the time."

Martha's sharp gaze flicked between Anders and Willa. "I assume this is about the men who robbed the bank and killed my husband?"

"It is," Anders replied, his voice steady and serious. "We've got a lead on where the gang's holed up. They're hiding out in a canyon north of here. It's a well-defended position, but I'm fixin' to gather a posse and flush them out."

Casey's jaw tightened, his hands clenching into fists at his side. "About time," he growled at Anders. "Where do we start?"

Willa swung down from her saddle, her boots hitting the ground with a thud. She stepped forward, her tone no-nonsense. "The canyon's got natural defenses—narrow entrance, steep walls. There's one main path in, and it's watched. I counted at least fifteen men when I scouted it, but there could be more. They've got sentries posted and a decent stash of supplies."

Tom, the younger of the two brothers, frowned. "Sounds like a death trap."

Willa shrugged. "Not if you've got enough men to make it look like hell's comin' for them."

Casey nodded, his expression resolute. "I can round up a dozen of our hands, maybe more if we pull some of the boys off the cattle. Give me a few hours to gather 'em, and we'll meet you at the Sheriff's office."

Anders tipped his hat. "Appreciate it, Casey. The more men we've got, the better."

As they turned to leave, Willa caught Casey's eye. "Make sure the men know what they're ridin' into," she said. "This ain't a cattle drive. These men won't hesitate to shoot."

Casey nodded grimly. "They'll be ready."

Back in Ironwood, Willa headed straight for the saloon. The Sheriff and his deputies were busy preparing supplies, and she knew she'd need a decent meal before the fight to come. She settled into a corner table, her eyes scanning the room as she ordered a plate of stew and a coffee.

The hours passed in a steady lull, but as the sun began to dip, the unmistakable thunder of hooves shattered the quiet. Willa set down her coffee and moved to the saloon door, stepping out onto the boardwalk.

A large group of riders was making its way down the main street toward the Sheriff's office. Casey and Tom rode at the front, their faces determined. Behind them came at least twenty men, their horses snorting and stamping as they pulled up outside the office.

Casey spotted Willa and tipped his hat before addressing Anders, who had come out to greet them. "We've got twenty good men," he said. "Some of 'em from our ranch, others from the Deep L. Hank Macey was a good friend of Pa's, and when he heard what we were doing, he sent his boys along."

Anders glanced at the assembled group, his expression approving. "That's a mghty fine turnout. Appreciate the support."

Casey swung down from his horse, his boots stirring the dust, and strode towards Anders. "We're ready when you are, Sheriff."

Willa stepped closer, her gaze sweeping over the group. The men looked tough and capable, their expressions grim with determination. She caught the Sheriff's eye and nodded. "Might just be enough to give us the edge we need."

Anders turned to the group, his voice firm and deadly serious. "Alright, listen up.

We're headin' out at first light. Make sure you've got enough ammunition and supplies to last a couple of days. We're not coming back until this is done."

The men murmured their agreement, some heading to the general store to stock up while others dismounted to stretch their legs. Willa watched them disperse, her mind already working through the plan ahead.

As the last rays of sunlight colored the sky in tints of gold and crimson, she turned to Anders. "You'd better hope they're as good as they look, Sheriff. Slade's gang ain't gonna go down easy."

Anders nodded, his jaw set. "They'll hold their own. The question is, will Slade's men?"

Willa smirked faintly. "Guess we'll find out."

CHAPTER TEN

Nash trailed the posse from the ridgeline, keeping his mare at a slow, deliberate pace. He'd promised Willa he'd stay put and wait for her, but he knew when he'd said this it was a lie. He needed to know if anyone was coming; if not, he'd need to work out his own plan. The sun was rising, casting a warm glow over the rugged terrain and illuminating the dust kicked up by the horses below. From his vantage point, he could see Anders leading the group with Willa riding close beside him. The Eldon boys and the ranch hands followed in a loose formation, their rifles slung across their saddles, eyes scanning the horizon with tense anticipation.

Nash's lips pressed into a thin line. Willa had done her part; she'd brought the sheriff and enough guns to make a stand. But it didn't mean things would go smoothly. Anders wasn't a fool, but Slade was a snake, and if they weren't careful, he'd slip right through their fingers.

As the posse wound their way through the narrow foothills leading toward the canyon, Nash kept his distance, careful to stay within the cover of the rocky terrain. The land was rough here, broken up by thick stands of juniper and patches of scrub that provided enough concealment to stay hidden. Nash's mare moved with steady precision, her hooves silent against the rocky ground.

Down below, Anders called for a halt, raising a gloved hand. The men fanned out, dismounting with wary glances toward the distant canyon. Nash watched as Willa dismounted gracefully, her rifle in hand, and joined Anders at the front. A few words were exchanged before the sheriff nodded and gestured for the men to begin setting up camp.

Nash rubbed his jaw, watching as the posse moved with the efficiency of men accustomed to long rides and hard fights. They were setting up camp well outside of Slade's range, choosing a small depression nestled between two hills. Smart. Anders wasn't about to ride in blind—he'd be taking the night to get his bearings, to plan, and to wait for the right moment.

Nash guided his mare down a rocky slope, careful to avoid drawing attention to himself. He needed a closer look at their camp without being seen. He tied his mare to a low-lying mesquite bush and crept forward on foot, his boots silent on the soft earth. From behind a cluster of boulders, he could make out the men as they built small fires, careful to keep them low and shielded from view. The scent of coffee drifted through the air, mingling with the familiar smell of horses and sweat.

Anders stood in the center of the camp, a map spread out on the ground in front of him, tracing his finger over it as Willa spoke, her brow furrowed in concentration. Nash couldn't hear their words, but he could tell from their expressions that they were discussing their approach. The Eldon boys loitered nearby, sharpening their knives and cleaning their rifles with quiet intensity.

Nash leaned back against the boulder, chewing over his next move. He could ride on and let them handle it, but something told him he needed to see this through; he needed Slade to clear his name.

As the light faded and the sounds of camp life quieted, Nash slipped back to his horse. He'd give them their space tonight, but come dawn, he planned to be close enough to lend a hand when the bullets started flying. He patted his mare's neck, whispering, "Get some rest, girl. We've got work to do come morning."

The night stretched long and quiet, the distant glow of the posse's campfires barely visible against the dark horizon. Nash settled into the saddle, his eyes fixed on the canyon ahead, knowing full well that by this time tomorrow, things would look a lot different.

As the first streaks of dawn stretched across the sky, the posse moved carefully through the rugged terrain surrounding the canyon. Nash, already in position, crouched low behind a rocky outcrop, his mare tethered safely behind a stand of scrub far enough away to avoid detection. His sharp eyes followed Anders and his men as they wound their way along the same treacherous path he and Willa had scouted earlier. It was a long, winding route, but it offered the advantage of height—if they could make it to the ridge unseen, they'd have Slade's men at their mercy.

Nash watched Willa near the front of the group, her rifle held loosely but ready, her keen gaze sweeping the landscape with practiced ease. Behind her, Anders moved with quiet purpose, signaling to his men to spread out and keep low. The Eldon boys were with them, their faces grim with anticipation, eager to mete out their brand of justice.

The path twisted and rose, the loose gravel underfoot forcing the posse to take slow, deliberate steps to avoid sending a cascade of noise down into the canyon below. Nash kept his breathing steady, his hand resting lightly on the hilt of his knife. Slade's lookouts were good. He knew they'd be posted up in the rocky crags and outcrops that lined the rim, watching for any sign of trouble.

As Anders and his men reached the last stretch of the ascent, Nash caught a flicker of movement further up the ridge. A figure emerged from the shadows, rifle in hand, his eyes sweeping the canyon edge below. Nash's muscles coiled. If the man turned his head even a fraction, he'd spot the posse closing in. The lookout shifted, the wind ruffling his scruffy beard as he yawned and rubbed his tired eyes. Nash took his chance.

Moving with the silent grace of a predator, he slipped from his cover and covered the distance in a few swift strides. The lookout barely had time to register his presence before Nash's knife flashed in the dim morning light. The blade sank deep and silent into the man's ribs, and Nash clamped a hand over his mouth, stifling the gurgled cry. He lowered the body to the ground gently, eyes scanning the canyon below to ensure no one had noticed.

From his position down the trail, Anders caught the movement and gave Nash a sharp nod, his expression a mixture of approval and wariness. Nash didn't nod back—no need. He wiped the blood from his knife on the lookout's shirt and crouched low, signaling to Anders to keep moving.

The men pressed on, their footsteps cautious, every rustle of wind through the brush making them pause. The canyon stretched out before them, and below, Slade's camp was just beginning to stir. Figures moved sluggishly among the tents, unaware of the danger creeping closer from above.

Nash fell in beside Willa as the posse reached the edge of the ridge. She glanced at him, raising a brow. "Quiet work," she murmured under her breath.

"Had to be," Nash muttered back, his eyes fixed on the camp below. "Let's hope it stays that way."

Anders gestured for everyone to take their positions, pointing out targets and signaling his men to ready their rifles. The tension thickened, the air growing still as the dawn's first light painted long shadows across the canyon floor.

Nash's fingers tightened around the grip of his Colt as he whispered, "It's gonna get real noisy soon."

And with that, the final preparations for the assault began.

Anders raised his hand, signaling the men to take their positions. A hush fell over them, the only sound the rustling of dry brush under shifting boots and the distant murmur of the outlaw camp below.

Nash, tucked away behind a rocky outcrop higher up the canyon wall, watched as Anders lined up his rifle, steadying the barrel against a weathered boulder. The sheriff's sights settled on the lone sentry standing near the camp's edge—a wiry man with a sharp, pockmarked face and a wild tangle of greasy hair beneath his battered hat. He wore a tattered duster, frayed at the edges, the once-dark fabric faded to a dusty brown. His spurs jangled faintly as he shifted his weight, oblivious to the eyes that tracked his every move.

'The sentry held a tin cup of coffee in one hand, steam curling lazily into the cool morning air. He took a slow sip, his eyes sweeping the camp above the rim of the tin cup. His other hand rested on the worn grip of the revolver at his hip, fingers idly tapping against the handle in a rhythmic pattern.

He yawned, stretching one arm lazily before taking another swig of coffee, his head tilting back just enough for Anders to see the full breadth of his chest.

The sheriff's finger tensed on the trigger.

Nash could almost hear the intake of breath before the shot cracked through the canyon, splitting the morning silence like a whip. The sentry jerked, his tin cup tumbling from his grasp, spilling dark liquid across the dirt as he staggered backward. A wet, choking sound escaped his lips as he crumpled, his body hitting the ground with a dull thud.

Anders' first shot shattered the dawn's stillness, echoing through the canyon like a crack of thunder. Nash's was the second, and it hit home with deadly precision—Nash's Colt barked once, and the sentry on the eastern ridge staggered back, his chest blossoming red before his legs gave out beneath him. The rifle he'd been holding slipped from his grasp, tumbling down the rocky slope. For a fleeting moment, his eyes were wide with shock, and then he crumpled like a marionette with its strings cut.

The gunshot sent ripples of chaos through the outlaw camp. A heartbeat of silence passed—then men erupted from their bedrolls and lean-tos, cursing and scrambling for their weapons, the flickering firelight casting frantic shadows across their weathered faces. Some dove for cover, thier actions chaotic, diving behind crates and overturned barrels, while others fumbled with their gun belts, confusion and fear thick in the air.

The gunshot shattered the morning stillness, sending ripples of chaos through the outlaw camp. For a heartbeat, everything stood still—the faint crackling of the dying campfire, the distant murmur of the wind against the canyon walls—before the camp erupted into pandemonium.

Men sprang from their bedrolls and lean-tos, shouts of alarm slicing through the air as they scrambled for their weapons. The flickering firelight painted their faces in erratic strokes, wide eyes, and clenched jaws thrown into sharp relief. Some dove headfirst behind crates and overturned barrels, knocking supplies and half-empty bottles into the dirt, while others fumbled with their gun belts, still sluggish with sleep, their hands shaking as they tried to load chambers with trembling fingers.

A tent collapsed as one outlaw bolted out too fast, dragging the canvas down with him in a tangled heap of ropes and fabric. He cursed and kicked his way free, knocking over a pot of coffee that hissed and spat as it hit the embers. The sharp tang of burning grounds mixed with the acrid scent of gunpowder as another round split the air, sending chunks of wood splintering from a wagon wheel.

A few men, their instincts sharper than their comrades, were already firing blindly, their bullets ricocheting off the canyon walls in sparks and echoes. The reports of gunfire bounced between the cliffs, making it impossible to tell where the shots were coming from. Horses tied at the edge of camp reared and snorted, their eyes rolling with panic, hooves striking against the rocky ground in a desperate bid for escape.

"Get the hell up!" a voice bellowed from within the chaos, cutting through the din. Slade.

He burst from the largest tent, his coat thrown hastily over his broad shoulders, his revolver already drawn. His eyes scanned the ridgeline above, his lips curling into a snarl. "They're on us, boys! Find cover and hold 'em off!"

Another outlaw sprinted past Slade, clutching a shotgun in his hands, only to be cut down mid-step, a burst of red spraying across the dirt as he crumpled with a ragged scream. The man next to him, younger and less experienced, dropped his rifle and bolted toward the horses, only to be tackled by another panicked outlaw, both of them hitting the ground in a heap of thrashing limbs and flailing fists.

Nash watched from above, his breath slow and measured despite the carnage below. He tracked the movement of the men, picking his targets carefully. Another shot rang out from Anders' position, taking down a man scrambling toward the ammunition cache. Nash allowed himself a small, grim nod—everything was going according to plan.

Across the ridge, Willa crouched low, rifle braced against her shoulder, her expression cold and steady as she fired with precision. She wasn't wasting bullets, each shot calculated and deliberate, and

Nash couldn't help but admire her skill even in the chaos.

The outlaws were in full retreat now, scurrying toward the makeshift barricades they had hastily thrown together—wagons flipped on their sides, sacks of supplies piled high—but the posse was closing in, their gunfire relentless. The canyon walls trapped the outlaws like penned cattle, their shouts turning to frantic, desperate cries as bullets found their marks.

Slade, still standing defiantly in the middle of it all, shouted orders that were swallowed by the chaos. His men, disorganized and terrified, were beginning to break apart. Nash could see it in their faces—the shift from fighting to fleeing.

The battle for the canyon was well underway, and Nash knew it wouldn't be long before the outlaws were finished. But there was still Slade, and Nash intended to make sure he didn't slip away in the confusion

The roar of gunfire echoed through the canyon, drowning out the shouts and panicked curses of Slade's men. Smoke curled in the hot morning air, thick and acrid, mingling with the scent of blood and dust. Nash moved like a shadow through the chaos, his Colt spitting fire with ruthless precision. His boots kicked up dirt as he ducked behind a broken supply wagon, pressing his back against the splintered wood, breath ragged but steady.

Across the camp, Slade stood in the midst of the turmoil, his face twisted with fury. "Hold your ground, damn it!" he snarled, shoving one of his men forward with enough force to send the poor bastard stumbling. "They ain't but ranch hands!" His voice was cracked with desperation, the bravado fading under the weight of their losses.

Nash wiped the sweat from his brow, his eyes narrowing as he watched Slade's ragged form through the swirling dust. The outlaw leader was doing everything he could to keep his men from breaking, barking orders, waving his gun, but Nash could see it—the doubt creeping in, the fear beneath the bravado. Slade was losing control.

Nash gritted his teeth. He wasn't here to see how long Slade could hold out. He was here to end this. He slid out from behind cover, his Colt raised, picking his targets with the cold efficiency of a man who'd been at this far too long. A shot rang out, and an outlaw crumpled near the fire pit, his pistol falling from limp fingers. Another turned to run but caught a bullet square in the back, falling face-first into the dirt.

Slade's head jerked around, his sharp eyes locking onto Nash through the thickening smoke. Even across the battlefield, Nash could see the flash of recognition in the outlaw's eyes; the hatred coiled there like a rattlesnake ready to strike.

"You son of a bitch!" Slade roared, firing wildly in Nash's direction. Bullets tore through the air, one zipping past Nash's ear so close he could feel the heat of it. He dropped low, rolling behind a stack of crates as splinters exploded around him.

Slade was dangerous, too dangerous to leave in the wind. But Nash needed him alive. A corpse wouldn't clear his name. He had to put him down hard enough to take the fight out of him without sending him to an early grave.

Slade peeked out, his gun ready, and Nash fired.

The bullet caught him in the shoulder with a sickening crack, and Slade reeled back, slamming against the barrels with a guttural cry. His revolver slipped from his fingers, landing with a dull thud in the dust. He clutched his wounded arm, blood seeping through his shirt, his face contorted in pain and fury.

For a moment, everything seemed to be still. Nash could hear the distant shouts of Anders and the Eldon boys pressing their attack, the pop of gunfire fading into the background. His eyes never left Slade, watching as the outlaw stumbled, his legs shaking under him.

Slade's gaze found Nash again, and despite the pain, he managed a ragged grin. "Ain't over yet," he spat, his voice hoarse.

Nash stepped forward, his Colt trained squarely on the outlaw's chest. "Yeah, it is," he said, his voice low and steady.

Slade's men hesitated, eyes darting to their wounded leader. Without his barked orders driving them forward, their resolve was crumbling. Some were already backing away, retreating toward the canyon's edge.

Anders had also seen Slade go down, and he didn't give them time to rethink. He fired another shot, striking the ground near their feet. "Slade's down. Drop your guns!" he barked, his voice cutting through the chaos like a whip crack. "It's over!"

Some hesitated, their hands twitching near their holsters, but when Anders and the Eldon boys advanced with rifles leveled, the choice became clear. One by one, the outlaws let their weapons clatter to the ground, their faces set in grim defeat.

Slade, still clutching his bleeding shoulder, glared at Anders with pure hatred. "You shoulda killed me," he spat, his voice ragged with pain.

Nash stepped forward, his expression hard. "Nah," he said coolly. "You're gonna do something much worse—you're gonna talk."

"Let's get him back to town," Anders said, looking at Nash. "Make sure he lives long enough to tell the truth. He'll get his day in court. But first, we need to patch him up."

Nash turned his gaze back to Willa. She was watching him, something unreadable in her expression. He gave her a slight nod, and she returned it with a smirk. "Guess you're goona prove to me you're not just a wanted drifter after all," she said coming to stand next to him.
Nash cracked a half-smile. "Never was."

With Slade groaning in pain and the remaining gang rounded up, Nash knew the fight wasn't over yet. But for the first time in a long while, it felt like he was on the right side of it.

Casey Eldon's sharp eyes landed on Nash, and the moment recognition set in, his rage boiled over like a dam breaking. "You!" he roared, his voice slicing through the canyon like a whip crack.

Nash barely had time to brace himself before Casey's fist crashed into his jaw, sending him stumbling back. Casey wasn't looking for a fight; he was looking for blood. And so was his brother. Tom came in hard, a vicious punch slamming into

Nash's ribs, the force of it ripping the breath from his lungs and making his knees buckle.

"Get up, you son of a bitch!" Casey snarled, seizing the front of Nash's shirt and yanking him upright just to drive another brutal blow across his face. Nash hit the ground like a sack of bricks, his body skidding in the dirt, and stars danced in his vision.

Boots crunched against the earth, closing in, and Tom's voice cut through the haze of pain. "You got my Pa killed," he spat. "And now you're gonna pay for it."

A boot drove into Nash's side, the impact detonating through his ribs like a firebrand. He curled slightly, but another kick followed, and then another, each one landing with sickening force. He gritted his teeth, biting down the groan and clawing its way up his throat. Fighting back was pointless—they'd kill him without hesitation if he gave them an excuse.

"Hold him up," Casey barked, his voice thick with fury.

Tom grabbed Nash by the collar, yanking him to his feet and shoving him forward. Nash's legs trembled under him, his battered body barely able to stand. Blood dripped steadily from a cut above his eye, staining the dry earth beneath him in dark rivulets.

The posse stood by, watching in uneasy silence. Some of them had grim satisfaction on their faces; others couldn't meet Nash's gaze. Sheriff Anders lingered at the edge, his jaw clenched, eyes dark with something that might have been reluctance—or regret. But he didn't step in. No one did.

Casey pulled his arm back again, his knuckles already raw and bloodied, murder flashing in his eyes.

And then—*crack!*

The rifle shot shattered the air, echoing through the canyon and bringing everything to a sudden, jarring halt. Casey froze mid-swing, his head snapping toward the source of the sound.

Willa stood atop a nearby rock, her rifle still aimed skyward, a thin wisp of smoke curling from the barrel. Her stance was rigid, eyes cold and sharp as flint. "That's enough," she said, her voice cutting through the heavy silence like a blade.

Casey's lip curled in defiance, his fists still clenched, but Willa took a step forward, leveling the rifle directly at him now. "I said enough," she repeated, the steel in her tone daring anyone to test her.

Tom took a hesitant step back, wiping sweat and dirt from his brow, but Casey wasn't so easily swayed. "You stay out of this, Callahan," he growled. "This ain't your fight."

"No," Willa said coolly, her eyes never leaving his. "It's the law's fight. And right now, you're about to cross a line you can't come back from."

Nash coughed, spitting blood into the dirt, and managed to lift his gaze to Willa. She didn't look at him, her focus locked on the Eldon brothers, her finger resting lightly on the trigger.

Anders finally stepped forward, placing a firm hand on Casey's shoulder. "Stand down, Casey," he ordered, his voice calm but firm. "We're not hangin' a man today."

Casey's chest rose and fell with ragged breaths, his nostrils flaring, but after a long moment, he released his grip on Nash's shirt, letting him crumple to the ground. "He ain't worth the rope anyway," Casey spat, backing off, but his eyes promised this wasn't over.

Willa lowered her rifle. She glanced down at Nash, her mouth a thin line. "You still alive?" she asked quietly.

Nash groaned, wiping at the blood trickling from his split lip. "Yeah," he rasped. "Thanks for the concern."

She rolled her eyes. "Don't make me regret it."

Anders barked orders to his men, and soon the tension in the canyon started to ease, the men dispersing, their anger simmering but contained for now.

Willa reached down, offering Nash a hand. He hesitated before taking it, his grip firm but unsteady. As she hauled him to his feet, she muttered under her breath, "Next time, try not to be such an easy target."

Nash smirked despite the pain. "I'll keep that in mind."

With Willa's help, Nash was half-dragged, half-carried to his horse. She pulled him up into the saddle with surprising strength, her hands lingering just long enough to make sure he wasn't going to fall off. "I'll be right behind you," she muttered, mounting her own horse.

Nash's body protested every movement, but he managed a rough nod. As they set off back toward town, he could feel Casey's glare digging into his back, and he knew this wasn't over—not by a long shot.

CHAPTER ELEVEN

The air inside the sheriff's office hung heavy and thick with the stench of sweat, gunpowder, and blood. The kind of tension that made a man feel like he was sitting on a lit powder keg. Nash sat on the edge of the narrow cot inside his cell, his ribs throbbing, every breath painful. Across from him, in the adjacent cell, Slade lounged like a man without a care in the world, his injured shoulder bound but still seeping through the cloth.

Sheriff Anders stood outside the bars, watching both of them with the weariness of a man who'd seen too much. His hand rested on the worn grip of his revolver, his eyes hard. Behind him, Doc Taylor worked with nervous hands, dabbing at Slade's wound with a shaking rag. Every so often, the Doc would glance toward Nash, clearly debating whether he should bother helping a man the whole town wanted to string up.

Slade's lips curled into that damnable smirk of his. "Well, look at us," he drawled, shifting against the cot with a groan. "Two sides of the same coin, huh? Both locked up, both bleedin', and neither one of us gettin' out anytime soon."

Nash didn't respond right away. He shifted his shoulders, wincing at the pull of bruised muscle. "Difference is," he said finally, his voice low and even, "I don't belong here."

Slade chuckled, the sound low and full of dark amusement. "Sure about that? Seems to me you got just as much blood on your hands as I do. The town thinks so, anyhow. Must eat at you, bein' stuck in here, knowin' they're outside with ropes in hand."

Anders cleared his throat, cutting through the tension. "Doc," he grunted, "patch Nash up next. I want him in one piece when the judge gets here."

Taylor hesitated, glancing at the sheriff. "You sure about that, Anders? Folks ain't gonna like it."

"Let me worry about the folks," Anders shot back. "Do your job."

Taylor sighed and walked over to Nash's cell, fishing gauze and salve from his worn leather bag. He unlocked the door with a begrudging look, stepping inside. Nash sat up straighter as the Doc went to work, pressing the bandages tighter around his ribs. He sucked in a quick breath through clenched teeth but didn't make a sound.

Slade watched with keen interest, a wolfish grin spreading across his face. "Bet that smarts, don't it?" He tilted his head.

"Musta been hell takin' that beatin'. Thought they were gonna kill ya right there."

Nash shot him a glare. "Still here, ain't I?"

"Yeah," Slade mused, resting his head back against the bars, "but for how long?" His grin widened. "Folks around here don't much care for justice, just revenge. And I reckon they're still lookin' to hang someone for old man Eldon."

Nash didn't answer; he just let the Doc finish his work, his thoughts racing. Willa was still out there, likely working to find a way to clear his name. He had to trust her to bring Anders around, but trust didn't come easy.

"Hold still," Taylor muttered, tightening the last of the bandages with more force than was needed.

Nash let out a slow breath as Taylor stepped back, gathering his things. "You're done," the Doc said, then turned toward the sheriff. "That good enough for you, Anders?"

Anders nodded. "That'll do."

The sheriff glanced between the two prisoners, his face unreadable. "One of you's guilty, maybe both. The judge'll figure it out. Until then, you keep your mouths shut and stay put."

As the sheriff turned and walked back to his desk, Slade leaned forward, gripping the bars with his good hand. "I gotta admit, Nash," he said, his voice lowering to something almost conversational, "I didn't think you'd still be breathin'. Thought Eldon's boys would've done you in proper."

Nash leaned back against the wall, letting his head rest against the cool iron bars. "You talk too much, Slade."

Slade laughed. "Maybe. But at least I ain't the one sittin' here thinkin' I can still walk outta this with a clean slate. Me, I know I'm gonna hang. No doubt about that. But you still got hope, and it's sad to see."

Nash said nothing, just stared at the ceiling, listening to the muffled sounds of the town outside. He knew his window to prove his innocence was closing fast.

As soon as the door creaked shut behind Sheriff Anders, Slade's smirk widened. He leaned forward, his fingers curling around the iron bars separating them. "Well, now," he drawled, his voice low and laced with amusement. "Looks like it's just you and me, Nash. Cozy, ain't it?"

Nash didn't respond, just shifted slightly on the cot, adjusting the bandage that was already rubbing raw against his ribs. His jaw was tight, his gaze fixed on the floorboards, but he could feel Slade's eyes crawling over him like a snake sizing up its next meal.

Slade chuckled, the sound deep and smug. "You know, I been thinkin'. Sheriff out there? He ain't the one holdin' your life in his hands." He tapped his chest with his good hand, grinning. "No, sir. That's all on me."

Nash flicked his eyes up, his expression unreadable.

Slade leaned closer, his voice dropping to a conspiratorial whisper. "I could tell Anders the truth; tell him you're just some poor drifter who stumbled into town at the wrong damn time. That you ain't got a lick of involvement in all this mess." He tilted his head, his grin turning downright wicked. "But tell me, Nash—why in the hell would I do a thing like that?"

Nash's fingers curled into a fist against his thigh, but he kept his face still, blank. Slade was fishing, looking for any crack he could widen.

Slade sighed theatrically and leaned back against the bars, stretching his legs out in front of him. "Nah, I figure you and me? We're gonna ride this one out together. I ain't one for dyin' alone, and I sure as hell ain't lettin' you walk out of here without me seein' that rope tighten 'round your neck."

Nash exhaled slowly, feeling the weight of Slade's words settle in his chest like a stone. He didn't have time for this. He didn't have time for Slade's games. He had to find a way out and fast.

Slade's grin never faltered. "You can glare all you want, cowboy. But deep down, you know I got you pinned in tighter than a hog in a pen. You got no friends in this town. Ain't no one comin' for you, 'cept maybe that lynch mob outside. And if they don't string you up first..." He let the thought hang, his laughter cold and sharp. "Well, you can always count on me."

Nash rolled his shoulders, feeling the burn in his bruised ribs but ignoring it. "You talk too much, Slade," he muttered again, his voice low but firm.

Slade's smirk widened. "And you don't talk enough, Nash. That's your problem."

The door creaked open, and Anders strode back in, adjusting his gun belt. His sharp eyes flicked between the two of them, suspicion suddenly darkening his face. "Something I should know about?"

Slade's smirk didn't waver. "Nothin', Sheriff," he said, smiling falsely. "Just chattin' with my new cellmate here. Ain't that right?"

Nash didn't answer. He just leaned back against the wall, his mind racing, but his face betraying nothing.

Anders studied them both a moment longer, then shook his head and went back to his desk. Slade chuckled softly, tapping the bars with a slow, taunting rhythm.

"Tick tock, Nash," he whispered. "Clock's windin' down."

Sheriff Anders stood by his desk, arms crossed, his eyes fixed on Nash with the tired wariness of a man who'd seen too much and trusted too little.

"You know you've got the wrong man, Sheriff," Nash said, his voice steady but edged with frustration. "I didn't kill Dan Elders. Slade's the one you want. You know his gang did the bank robbery."

Slade let out a low chuckle, tipping his head back against the bars. "Now, that ain't very friendly, Nash. Accusin' me like that without a shred of proof. I'm wounded."

Anders' eyes flicked to Slade, then back to Nash, his expression unmoved. "That might be so? Do you have anything to back that up? Men say they saw you shoot old man Eldon, that you were part of Slade's outfit."

Nash shifted, wincing as the movement sent a sharp ache through his ribs. "I was on the trail when Elders was shot. Hell, half the town saw me ride in after it happened. Slade and his boys were the ones on the run."

Anders sighed, rubbing at the back of his neck. "I don't deal in what-ifs, Nash. What I got is a town full of angry men who say you fit the description, and no one saw Slade pull the trigger."

Nash clenched his jaw, frustration simmering beneath his calm exterior. "There were people in the bank, surely they saw who made the shot?"

Anders shook his head. "Gang had bandanas over their faces, only clear face anyone seen was yours."

"I wasn't in the bank, ask the witnesses who were there" Nash protested, feeing his anger rising.

The sheriff's face hardened. "I got a widow and two sons cryin' for blood and a town that wants to see justice served. Ain't much choice in it, Nash."

Slade grinned, leaning forward to rest his elbows on his knees. "Face it, Nash. You're the perfect scapegoat. Drifter rolls into town, and trouble follows. Folks don't ask too many questions when things line up too easy." He clicked his tongue, shaking his head. "Me, though? I'm a survivor. I know how to play my cards."

Nash's fists curled at his sides, but he kept his tone even. "You're a murderer, Slade. You shot Elders down in cold blood, and you know it."

Slade's smile didn't falter. "Maybe I did. Maybe I didn't. Don't much matter, does it? 'Cause right now, the good sheriff here's got you locked up for that instead of me."

Anders sighed heavily, pacing a few steps before turning back to Nash. "Even if I believed you, without a confession or some hard proof, my hands are tied. The judge'll be here in a few days, and until then, you're stayin' put."

Nash sat back against the cold iron bars, his jaw tight. He knew Anders was telling the truth, but it didn't make the situation any easier to swallow. Slade wasn't about to confess, and without that, Nash was nothing but a convenient fall guy.

Anders studied him for a long moment, his brow furrowed. "You say Slade's my man, Nash? Then, you better find a way to prove it before the rope tightens around your neck. Sure, we can pin the bank job on him, but we got witnesses say you were the one who killed Dan Elders."

Nash didn't answer right away; just let his eyes drift to Slade, who was watching him like a cat eyeing a trapped mouse. Nash's gut told him one thing—he had to make Slade slip up, had to push him hard enough to crack that cool, smug façade. But time was running out.

"You still got friends out there, Nash?" Anders asked, his voice quieter now.

Nash's gaze didn't waver. "Maybe. But I wouldn't count on 'em showing up in time."

Anders nodded, then turned back to his desk, leaving Nash and Slade alone again.

Slade smirked and leaned back, lacing his fingers behind his head. "Clock's tickin', Nash. Hope you got a plan, 'cause I ain't much for sharin' the blame."

Nash watched him, his mind already working through his next move. He wasn't about to hang for another man's crime. One way or another, he'd see this through.

The sheriff's office smelled of stale sweat and gun oil, the kind of scent that clung to the walls like a bad memory. Nash sat on the narrow cot, his arms resting on his knees, staring at nothing in particular. The weight of the situation pressed heavy on his chest, and the ache in his ribs didn't help matters much. The sound of boots on the wooden floor pulled him from his thoughts, and when he looked up, Willa was standing just inside the doorway, holding a bottle of whiskey in one hand.

Sheriff Anders looked her over, his expression wary. "What's this now?"

"Just thought he might want a drink," Willa said, lifting the bottle slightly. Her tone was casual, but there was an edge beneath it, the same edge Nash had come to recognize as her way of saying she wasn't taking no for an answer.

Anders grunted, shifting his weight. "Long as he doesn't make trouble, I suppose it's fine."

Willa shot Nash a look as she stepped closer to his cell, holding the bottle out through the bars. "Figured you could use this," she said, her eyes flickering over him like she was trying to gauge how bad off he really was.

Nash reached through the bars, taking the bottle from her with a nod. "Obliged," he said, his voice rough from too much dust and not enough rest.

Before he could say anything more, Slade's voice cut through the room like a rusted blade. "Ain't that sweet," he drawled from his cell, pushing himself up from the cot with a grin. "The lady bringin' her man a drink like somethin' outta one of those dime novels."

Willa didn't acknowledge him, but Nash saw the way her jaw tightened, the way her grip shifted on the Colt at her hip. Slade wasn't one to let things go, though. He sauntered up to the bars, his fingers curling around the iron as he leered at her. "Maybe you should bring me one too, sweetheart," he said, his grin widening. "Could get awful thirsty in here with all this talk of justice and hangings."

Nash saw it coming a second before it happened—the flicker in Willa's eyes, the shift in her stance. Before Slade could even think about moving out of the way, the butt of her Colt smashed hard against his knuckles, sending him staggering back with a string of curses. He clutched his hand to his chest, blood trickling from split skin, his expression shifting from cocky amusement to seething anger.

"Oops," Willa said flatly, her face hard as stone. "Didn't see you there."

Slade's eyes burned with fury, but before he could get a word out, Anders was there, his voice sharp and filled with authority. "That's enough!" He pointed a finger at Willa, his face dark with irritation. "You're done here. Get out."

Willa straightened, brushing imaginary dust off her jacket, and turned toward the door without a word. But before stepping outside, she glanced back at Nash, something unspoken passing between them. "Don't drink it all at once," she said with a smirk, then walked out, her boots clicking against the wooden planks.

Anders shook his head, running a hand down his face. "I swear, this town's gonna be the death of me." He shot Nash a hard look. "You cause any trouble, and I'll be the one smashing skulls next time."

Nash lifted the whiskey bottle in a mock toast. "Wouldn't dream of it, Sheriff."

Slade sat back down on his cot, scowling at his hand and muttering under his breath. Nash just leaned against the bars, taking a long, slow pull from the bottle. The whiskey burned all the way down, but it was a welcome distraction from the pain—both the physical and the kind that ran deeper.

Outside, the sound of Willa's spurs faded into the night, but the ghost of her presence lingered. Nash wasn't sure what game she was playing, but he had a feeling she wasn't done with him just yet.

CHAPTER TWELVE

The jailhouse was quiet. Anders had left to calm the Eldon family down, and the only sounds now were the rhythmic creak of the sheriff's chair and the occasional cough from the deputy who was now seated in it. The streets of Ironwood outside had settled into an uneasy silence, the earlier tension still thick in the air. Nash lay on his cot, staring at the ceiling, his ribs aching with every breath. Sleep wasn't coming easy—not with Slade in the next cell and the whole town still half-convinced he was guilty.

A low, ragged cough cut through the stillness. Slade shifted on his cot, groaning in pain. "Hey," he rasped, barely above a whisper. "Sheriff… somethin' ain't right."

The deputy on duty, a wiry young man named Franklin, looked up from his chair with a frown. "What now?"

Slade groaned again, doubling over, his face contorted in pain. "That damn wound… it's gone bad. Feels like fire. It's bleedin' real bad." He sagged against the bars, his breathing ragged and shallow. "I—I can't breathe…"

Franklin hesitated, shifting his rifle. "You're fine. Anders had the doc look at you earlier."

Slade gagged, coughing violently and retching onto the floor; a moment later, he collapsed. Franklin muttered a curse and strode toward the cell, unlocking it cautiously.

"Don't," Nash warned a second too late.

It was a mistake.

In a blur of movement, Slade sprung up from the floor, his good arm snaking around Franklin's throat. The deputy choked out a strangled cry as Slade wrenched his sidearm from its holster and shoved the barrel against his ribs.

"Now," Slade growled, his earlier weakness gone. "We're gonna take a little walk."

Franklin, wide-eyed and panicked, stumbled forward, forced out of the cell by Slade's relentless grip. The door creaked, and Anders stepped in. He blinked, eyes going wide, when he saw Slade with the gun.

"Drop it, Sheriff," Slade barked, backing toward the door, Franklin still in front of him like a human shield. "Or your boy here gets his guts spilled."

Anders, frozen for a beat, reluctantly let his revolver fall to the desk. Slade grinned. Slade's grip on Franklin tightened, the gun pressing hard against the young deputy's ribs as he backed toward the cells. His grin was sharp, teeth flashing in the dim light of the jailhouse. "Go on, Sheriff," he said, nodding toward the open cell door. "Get in. I'd hate to have to clean your boy's blood off my boots."

Anders hesitated, his jaw working, but the look in Franklin's wide, terrified eyes told him he didn't have much of a choice. Slowly, the sheriff stepped inside the empty cell, hands raised in a gesture of reluctant surrender. Slade chuckled darkly, his eyes flicking to Franklin, and then he pushed the boy toward the cell. "Your turn now, get it and lock it up, nice and tight. Then throw the keys out here."

Franklin swallowed hard, his hands trembling as he fumbled with the keys at his belt. Slade's patience was razor-thin, and he gave the deputy a shove. "Come on, boy, I ain't got all night."

With a sharp *click*, the cell door swung shut, and Franklin tossed the keys out onto the floor at Slade's feet. Anders wrapped his hands around the bars, glaring at Slade with the kind of quiet fury that promised retribution. "You're makin' a mistake, Slade."

Slade leaned in, his breath reeking. "Mistake?" he sneered. "No, Sheriff. You made the mistake." He tapped a finger against the iron bars, enjoying himself.

"You should've listened to the drifter here. He didn't shoot Elders." His grin widened, a glint of satisfaction in his dark eyes. "I did. Square in the chest. The bullet hit him so hard, it lifted him right off his damn feet and sent him flyin' back through those fancy bank doors like a rag doll." He laughed, shaking his head. "Hell, I can still see the look on his face."

Nash, standing in the neighboring cell, his hands resting on the bars, met Anders' gaze with cold eyes. "Well, Sheriff," he drawled, "looks like you got the truth of the matter now."

Anders' lips pressed into a thin line, his eyes burning with quiet anger. "Yeah," he muttered, his voice low and dangerous. "I reckon I do."

Slade, still gloating, disappeared out into the night, the jailhouse door swinging shut behind him. The heavy silence that followed was only broken by the soft jingle of spurs as Nash shifted his weight.

Anders' shoulders slumped slightly, his hands still gripping the bars, but then, with a slow grin creeping across his face, he reached into his coat and pulled out a set of keys.

Nash raised an eyebrow. "Well, I'll be damned," he said, watching as Anders calmly unlocked the cell door and stepped out.

"Always keep a spare," Anders muttered, shaking his head. "Never did trust Franklin with the only set." He glanced over at Nash before tossing him the keys. "Now, let's go get that son of a bitch."

Nash caught the keys. "Took you long enough, Sheriff."

Anders retrieved his rifle from the desk where he'd left it and checked the chamber with practiced ease. "You're awful cocky for a man just sprung from a jail cell."

Nash shrugged. "Well, Sheriff, I figure I ain't got much to lose." He reached for his Henry still propped against the jailhouse wall. "Now, let's see if we can't catch up to Slade before he gets too far."

Anders pulled open a draw and held out Nash's gunbelt with his Colt. Then, stepping toward the door, his expression grim and determined. "You're right about that, Nash. No more mistakes."

Nash and Anders strode out of the jailhouse, the heavy door swinging shut behind them with a dull *thud.* The night air was cool, and the town of Ironwood stood still, shrouded in uneasy silence. Anders didn't break stride as he turned to Franklin, who stood pale-faced near the jail's steps.

"Franklin," Anders barked, his voice sharp and commanding. "You get your ass moving and raise the alarm. Tell the Eldon boys what's happened, and get every man who can hold a gun ready to ride."

Franklin swallowed hard, nodding quickly. "Yes, sir," he stammered before bolting down the street toward the Eldon ranch hands, his boots kicking up dust in his wake.

Anders turned to Nash, sizing him up with a glance. "You gonna be able to keep up, drifter?"

Nash smirked faintly, the whiskey Willa had brought him still buzzing through his veins, dulling the ache in his ribs just enough to make the saddle bearable. "I'll manage," he muttered, pulling himself into the saddle with a grunt. His mare shifted beneath him, sensing his tension, but Nash gave her a steadying pat. "Besides, I ain't the one who let Slade walk out."

Anders scowled, swinging onto his own horse with a practiced ease. "Don't push your luck. Let's just get the bastard before he gets too far."

As they galloped down Ironwood's main street, lanterns flickered to life in the windows of the saloon and general store, curious faces peeking through curtains. Nash's sharp eyes scanned the darkness ahead, muscles tense, heart pounding in his chest with a mix of anticipation and frustration.

Near the edge of town, a man stood outside his house, fumbling to light his lamp. Anders reined in hard beside him, the sheriff's voice cutting through the night like a whip. "You seen anyone come through here?"

The man squinted up at them, the glow of the freshly lit lamp flickering across his face. "Yeah," he grunted, jerking his thumb toward the dark stretch of road leading west. "Took off like a scalded cat 'bout ten minutes ago. Headed that way, fast."

Anders gave a curt nod. "Much obliged." Without another word, he spurred his horse forward, Nash right behind him.

The trail stretched ahead, bathed in the dim silver light of the moon. Their horses pounded the dirt hard, hooves kicking up dust that hung in the air behind them. Nash's gaze flicked to the ground, scanning for tracks. The faint imprint of horseshoes stood out in the soft patches of earth, and he could tell Slade was pushing his mount hard.

"He's riding like a man with the devil on his heels," Nash called over the thundering hooves.

Anders grunted. "That's because he knows we'll string him up before sunrise if we catch him."

Nash's lips twitched into something that wasn't quite a smile. "Then we best not keep him waiting."

They pressed on, the wind biting at their faces, and Nash felt the familiar rush of the chase settle deep into his bones. One way or another, this would end tonight.

The rhythmic pounding of hooves echoed through the vast emptiness of the open range, a relentless drumming against the hard-packed earth. The moon, full and round, cast a pale silver glow over the rolling hills and jagged outcrops, painting the landscape in sharp contrasts of light and shadow. Nash felt the sting of the cold night air against his face; it kept him, altert, the wind whipping at his coat and tugging at the brim of his hat. Dust billowed beneath the horses' hooves, rising in ghostly clouds that swirled and vanished into the dark.

Ahead of them, the faint silhouette of Slade's retreating figure darted between the rocks and sparse brush, always just out of reach. His horse, lathered and struggling, stumbled briefly before finding its footing again, but Nash could see the signs—Slade was pushing too hard, too fast. The trail he left behind was ragged, hoof prints scattered and uneven, the telltale marks of a desperate man running out of road.

Anders rode hard beside him, his jaw set tight, eyes fixed on the fugitive ahead. His rifle bounced against his saddle, and every few moments, his fingers twitched as if itching to pull it free. The sheriff's horse, a sturdy bay, snorted steam into the cool night, its muscles bunching with every stride.

"Trail's getting rough," Nash called over the wind. His eyes swept the land ahead, taking in the narrowing gap between the hills where Slade was headed. "He's running blind."

Anders grunted in response, urging his horse faster. "He's cornered, just don't know it yet."

The terrain grew even more treacherous, the ground littered with loose shale and low-lying shrubs that clawed at the horses' legs, threatening to make the animal stumble. Nash felt his horse shift beneath him, the mare adjusting instinctively, her hooves finding purchase with practiced ease. He leaned low, pressing close to her neck, feeling the heat radiate off her sweat-slicked coat.

The faint howl of a coyote echoed somewhere in the distance, a lonely sound swallowed quickly by the wind. Nash flicked a glance toward the horizon. Dawn was creeping in slowly, an orange sliver stretching across the eastern sky. Time was running short, and the longer Slade stayed ahead, the harder it would be to catch him before he vanished into the unforgiving wilderness beyond.

"Cut him off at the ridge," Nash called out, angling his mare toward a rocky incline to the right. "He won't make it through the pass."

Anders nodded and veered left, their plan wordless but understood. Nash pushed his horse harder, feeling the strain in her stride, the rapid heave of her breaths as she climbed the slope. Rocks skittered down beneath her hooves, tumbling into the darkness below, but he didn't slow. The ridge offered higher ground—a vantage point that could mean the difference between catching Slade or losing him for good.

As he crested the rise, Nash pulled his mare to a halt, scanning the dark stretch below. Slade was out there, riding recklessly through the canyon, his horse laboring under the strain, tired and nearing the end. Nash raised a hand, signaling to Anders below.

The sheriff raised his rifle in silent acknowledgment.

Nash's grip tightened on the reins, his eyes narrowing. "No more running, Slade," he muttered under his breath. With a sharp kick, he urged his mare forward, ready to end this chase once and for all.

CHAPTER THIRTEEN

The first hints of dawn crept over the horizon, streaking the sky with pale hues of pink and gold. Nash and Anders had slowed their horses to a cautious walk, their eyes scanning the trail ahead. The dirt path stretched out before them, the hoofprints of Slade's mount becoming more erratic, uneven, and desperate.

Nash tugged gently on the reins, raising his hand in a silent signal to Anders. The sheriff pulled up alongside him, his rifle resting across his saddle horn, eyes sharp beneath the brim of his hat.

"He's close," Nash said quietly, his voice carrying just enough edge to make Anders sit up straighter. He pointed to the fresh, scattered tracks in the loose earth. "See that? His horse is faltering. He's pushed it too hard—stumbled a couple of times already. He'll be lookin' for a place to hole up." Nash narrowed his eyes, scanning the low hills and clusters of scrub ahead. "Trail's easy to follow, but don't get too comfortable. Slade knows we're comin'. He'll be watchin' for us just as much as we're watchin' for him."

Anders shifted in the saddle, his jaw set tight. "Man like Slade won't go down easy," he muttered, checking the load in his rifle. "But I aim to make damn sure he does."

Nash's eyes flicked to the sheriff, his lips pressing into a thin line. "Good," he said simply, before nudging his mare forward, keeping to the edge of the trail where the brush provided some cover.

They moved slowly now, both men silent but alert. The landscape stretched ahead in rolling swells of dry earth and scattered rock formations, the kind of place a man could vanish into if he knew what he was doing. Nash kept his eyes low, watching the tracks carefully. They were leading up toward a ridge that overlooked the trail, a good spot for an ambush. His gut told him Slade wasn't done fighting yet.

Anders scanned the horizon with a practiced eye. "Reckon he's settin' up to take us from higher ground?"

Nash nodded grimly. "That's what I'd do. He's got nothin' left but his gun and his nerve, and that's when men like him are at their worst." He pulled his Colt from his belt, checking the cylinder before settling it back. "Keep your rifle handy, Sheriff. This could turn ugly real quick."

Anders grunted, shifting his weight in the saddle. "It already is."

They pressed on, their horses' hooves muffled in the soft earth. A faint breeze rustled through the brush, carrying the distant caw of a crow. Nash could feel it in his bones—Slade was near, and he was waiting.

As they rounded a bend, Nash held up a hand again, this time lower and more urgent. He slid from his saddle, crouching down to inspect a disturbed patch of dirt near a cluster of low boulders. "Fresh," he muttered, running his fingers through the churned-up earth. "Could be where he bailed off his horse."

Anders dismounted as well, his rifle at the ready. "So what now?"

Nash straightened slowly, his eyes scanning the jagged ridge just beyond. "Now we make sure we ain't the ones walkin' into a bullet." He gestured to a narrow outcrop leading up the ridge. "We take it slow, keep to the shadows."

Anders nodded, and they moved forward on foot, their boots crunching softly against the dry ground. Every step was measured, every movement deliberate. Nash's pulse was steady, but his senses were razor-sharp. Slade was close, and when they found him, it wouldn't be pretty.

The sharp crack of the rifle shattered the still morning air, the echo rolling through the canyon like distant thunder. Instinct took over before thought could catch up—Nash threw himself into the dust, his body hitting the hard-packed ground with a jarring impact that sent pain exploding through his ribs. White-hot agony seared through his chest, and for a moment, he couldn't breathe, couldn't move, pinned under the weight of his own battered body. He gritted his teeth, swallowing the groan that threatened to escape, his vision swimming with the effort to stay conscious.

Dust swirled around him, thick and choking, settling in the creases of his coat and stinging his eyes. He forced himself onto his side, gasping shallow breaths that did little to ease the fire in his ribs. Every inhale felt like a blade twisting in his chest, but he shoved the pain aside—there'd be time to deal with it later, if he survived this.

The spot where he'd been standing moments ago was now pockmarked with bullet holes, the ground torn up by the shot that had nearly found its mark. Nash clenched his jaw, pressing a hand against his side as if to hold himself together, and glanced toward the ridge. His eyes narrowed, scanning the rocks for movement. He knew Slade was out there, watching, waiting. Nash's fingers curled around the grip of his Colt, sweat slicking his palm despite the morning chill.

He couldn't afford to stay down for long. Gritting his teeth against the raw pain, Nash pushed himself up to a crouch, every movement sending fresh jolts of agony through his battered ribs. But he kept going—he had no other choice. Turning back toward Anders, Nash's stomach clenched. The sheriff lay sprawled in the dirt, his chest rising and falling in ragged jerks, but his rifle lay abandoned at his side, forgotten. Blood soaked into his shirt, dark and spreading.

"Damn it," Nash muttered, his fingers curling tight around his Colt.

A low, taunting voice carried across the canyon, bouncing off the rocks and filling the empty space between them. "It's just you and me now, Nash," Slade's voice drawled, thick with satisfaction. "Looks like your friend the sheriff ain't gonna be much help no more. You're all alone, boy."

Nash's gaze snapped to Anders, sprawled in the dirt, his chest heaving with ragged, uneven breaths. Blood seeped into his shirt, dark and spreading, and his rifle lay discarded at his side, useless. Nash's jaw tightened, his fingers flexing around the grip of his Colt. Every instinct screamed at him to go to the sheriff, to drag him to cover and make sure he wasn't dying. But Nash didn't move. He couldn't.

Slade was out there, watching, waiting. If Nash broke cover now, he'd be walking straight into a bullet. The outlaw had the high ground, and Nash knew damn well Slade wouldn't miss a second time. The only way to help Anders was to end this fast.

"Get this done," Nash muttered under his breath, shifting his weight and scanning the rocks with sharp, deliberate eyes. Slade was dug in somewhere, and Nash needed to find him—needed a clean shot before the outlaw had a chance to finish what he started. Nash gritted his teeth, forcing himself to stay low, to move slow and careful, his eyes searching every shadow, every crevice. He couldn't afford to rush. One wrong step, and Slade would have him dead to rights.

The sheriff groaned weakly, and Nash's gut twisted. He couldn't think about that now. If he didn't find Slade first, they'd both be corpses before the sun climbed much higher. Steeling himself, he pressed on, creeping along the rocks, his finger resting light on the trigger. Slade was out there—and Nash aimed to end this.

Nash's jaw tightened, his eyes scanning the rocky terrain. He had a good idea where the shot had come from—a cluster of jagged rocks up on the ridge, offering plenty of cover and a good line of sight, and he had the advantage of high ground. Keeping low, Nash edged around the boulder, his gaze flicking between Anders and the spot where Slade was likely holed up. The whiskey he'd downed earlier was losing its grip, and the pain in his ribs gnawed at him like a relentless buzzard. He pressed a hand against his side, feeling the heat radiating beneath the bandages.

Another shot cracked, sending a chunk of rock splintering off inches from Nash's head. He ducked lower, his pulse hammering against his ribs. Slade was taking his time, savoring the hunt.

"You ain't got nowhere to run, Nash," Slade called out, the grin in his voice clear as day. "Come on now, let's finish this."

Nash wiped a sleeve across his brow, the sweat slick against his skin. Hard and slow, that's how it was going to be. No charging in, no easy way out. Slade wanted to draw him out, make it personal, and Nash had no intention of giving him the satisfaction.

He took a deep breath and began inching his way around the outer edge of the canyon wall, sticking to the shadowed crevices where the light hadn't yet fully reached. Step by step, he closed the gap, his boots barely making a sound on the loose dirt. The trick was patience—outlasting Slade, making him think he was in control.

Another shot rang out, this one wider, hitting a rock well behind Nash. Slade was getting nervous, firing blind.

"You're slippin', Slade," Nash called out, his voice cool and even. "Missed by a mile."

Slade barked a laugh. "Ain't no hurry, Nash. I got all the time in the world. Question is, how much you got left?"

Nash ignored Slade's taunts, his focus narrowing to the space ahead, each step calculated, deliberate. The canyon was silent save for the whisper of wind threading through the rocks and the slow, measured crunch of his boots on gravel. He could feel the weight of his revolver against his hip, every fiber of his being itching to draw it, but he held steady, waiting for the right moment.

He moved low, hugging the rock face, his breath coming slow and steady. He could hear Slade up ahead—the slight shift of weight, the scrape of boot leather against stone as the outlaw adjusted his position. Nash's eyes tracked a break in the rocks, a narrow slit where the shadows pooled deeper, and there—just barely—a glint of steel catching the early morning sun.

He was close now. Close enough to smell the acrid tang of gunpowder lingering in the air. Close enough to feel the tension, thick and electric, hanging between them.

Another step, and Slade's voice cut through the quiet, laced with something that almost sounded like nervousness.

"You're a stubborn bastard, I'll give you that."

Nash didn't answer. He just kept moving, his body coiled tight with readiness. He shifted behind a boulder, his fingers curling slowly around the worn grip of his Colt. He could feel the sweat on his palm, the leather warm from the heat of his body.

Then—movement. A flash of motion in the shadows.

Slade fired.

The crack of the gunshot shattered the silence, the bullet slicing through the air so close Nash felt the heat of it kiss his cheek. He lunged forward, rolling into cover behind another outcrop of rock, his heart pounding in his chest but his hands steady as ever. Dust rained down from above where the shot had hit, but Nash barely noticed.

Slade was still hidden, but Nash had seen enough. He lined up his Colt, aiming for the faint gleam of metal nestled between the rocks, and squeezed the trigger.

The canyon echoed with the gunshot, a thunderous boom that sent birds scattering from the cliffs above. A sharp grunt of pain followed, and Nash knew he'd hit his mark.

He didn't give Slade a chance to recover. He moved fast, staying low, weaving between the rocks as he closed the distance. Slade's breathing was ragged now, labored, but Nash knew better than to think he was out of the fight. The outlaw was dangerous even when wounded.

Nash crept closer, his grip tightening on his Colt, his eyes scanning every shadow. Slade's figure came into view, slumped against the rock, his gun hand twitching, slick with blood.

Nash leveled his Colt. "End of the trail, Slade."

Slade's eyes flickered, his lips curling into a grimace. "Took you long enough," he rasped.

Nash didn't smile. He just steadied his aim and took another step forward, ready to finish what he'd started.

"Looks like you got a little bite left after all," Slade rasped, panting.

Nash stepped closer, his Colt leveled, his voice steady. "You're done, Slade. Drop it."

Slade's eyes darted around, looking for an out, but Nash had him boxed in. The outlaw let out a slow chuckle, shaking his head. "You think takin' me in's gonna fix everything? You and me both know some men ain't meant for the rope."

Nash's eyes hardened, and his finger tightened on the trigger. "Drop it," he said again, his voice cold as steel.

Slade's hand hovered over his belt, hesitation flickering across his face.

"Try it," Nash warned. "See what happens."

Slade licked his lips, his fingers twitching once, twice—and then he let the rifle slip from his grasp, the metal clattering against the rocks.

Nash didn't lower his gun. "Get up. Slow."

Slade staggered to his feet, his eyes still gleaming with that same damn arrogance, like he thought the fight wasn't over yet. Nash wasn't about to give him the chance to prove it otherwise. Behind him, the sound of hooves echoed down the trail, and Nash glanced back just long enough to see Anders, still alive, riding toward them, his face pale but determined.

Nash turned back to Slade, his jaw tight. "Looks like you're out of luck, Slade."

CHAPTER FOURTEEN

The distant sound of hooves pounded against the earth, growing louder with every heartbeat. Nash squinted against the glare of the rising sun, watching the approaching dust cloud rolling in like a storm. The posse was coming—Casey and Tom Eldon leading the charge, with Willa close behind them.

Nash felt a flicker of relief stir in his chest. He'd been holding his breath too long, waiting with his eyes locked on Slade, his revolver never wavering. The outlaw was wounded, slumped against the rock, his breathing ragged, but Nash knew better than to take his focus off him for even a second. Now, with help nearly there, the weight of the past few hours pressed down hard.

Slade must have heard the posse, too. He shifted, wincing, and let out a low chuckle, though it came strained through clenched teeth. "Looks like your friends finally decided to show," he rasped, blood trickling from the corner of his mouth.

Nash said nothing, his grip on the Colt steady, but there was a flicker of satisfaction in his gaze. He could already see Willa's horse pulling ahead of the others, her rifle resting easy across her saddle, her eyes scanning the rocky terrain. Behind her, the Eldon brothers rode hard, their jaws set in grim determination. Fraser, the deputy, rode alongside them, his face flushed with urgency, no doubt eager to prove himself after raising the alarm back in town.

As the riders drew closer, Nash let out a slow breath and allowed himself, for the first time, to relax his trigger finger. The waiting was nearly over.

The posse came to a halt in a cloud of dust and noise. Casey Eldon wasted no time, swinging down from his horse and stalking over to Nash with fire in his eyes. He barely spared him a glance before his gaze locked on Slade. "You son of a bitch," he growled, his voice thick with rage.

Tom joined him, his fists clenched at his sides. "We oughta finish what he started," he spat, looking at Nash.

"Not yet," Willa cut in, dismounting with a practiced ease. "The sheriff wants him alive." Her eyes flicked to Nash, taking in his battered state with a knowing look. "You holdin' up?"

Nash gave a slight nod, ignoring the ache in his ribs. "I'll live."

Casey and Tom didn't wait for any more discussion. They grabbed Slade roughly by the arms, dragging him to his feet and shoving him hard against his own horse. Slade groaned, his smirk fading as they yanked his hands behind his back and secured them with a length of rope.

"You Eldon boys ain't got much for manners," Slade sneered, his voice weaker than before.

Tom responded by shoving him face down over the saddle, earning another pained grunt. "That's for my Pa," he muttered under his breath, and Nash didn't blame him one bit.

The tension hung thick, but Anders' voice cut through it all as he reined in his horse. "Let's get him back to Ironwood," he ordered. "Judge Guttridge'll be here soon enough, and I want this bastard under lock and key before sundown."

Slade groaned again as his horse was led forward, tired and stumbling slightly under the weight. Nash watched the outlaw carefully, every movement filled with the desperate energy of a man who knew his time was running out.

Fraser, his earlier nervousness replaced with a bit more confidence, rode up alongside Nash. "You did good," he muttered. "Might've saved the town a whole lot of trouble."

Nash only grunted in response, watching as Willa walked her horse alongside him. She tossed him a canteen, which he caught with a nod of thanks. "You're lookin' worse for wear," she said.

Nash wiped the sweat from his brow with his sleeve, taking a deep pull from the water. "Feel worse, too."

Willa smirked. "Yeah, well, you ain't got time to lie down and die just yet. Sheriff's still got questions, and I reckon you'll want to see Slade hang."

Nash swallowed hard and capped the canteen. "Reckon I do."

Nash followed behind, his eyes locked on the town ahead, where justice—one way or another—was waiting. He rode in silence, one hand clutching the whiskey bottle someone had shoved into his grip, the other resting gingerly against his aching ribs. The pain in his side had settled into a dull throb, but he knew the worst was yet to come. Every jolt of his horse sent a sharp reminder through his battered body. He took a swig from the bottle, the burn of the liquor spreading warmth through his chest. It didn't do much to dull the ache, but it was better than nothing.

Behind him, Willa rode alongside Sheriff Anders, who kept his injured arm stiff at his side while Willa fussed over him, tearing a strip from her shirt to wrap it tight around his bleeding shoulder. Anders grunted, shooting her a glare.

"I told you, I ain't made of glass," he muttered.

"You ain't made of stone, either," Willa shot back, tightening the bandage with a sharp tug that made the sheriff hiss through his teeth.

Tom Eldon let out a humorless laugh. "You oughta let her patch you up proper, Sheriff. If you bleed out on us, who's gonna keep our friend Nash here from skippin' town?"

Nash glanced at Tom with a tired glare but didn't rise to the bait. He had no energy left for smart remarks. He just wanted to get back, put Slade behind bars for good, and finally rest.

Ironwood came into view as the sky turned shades of deep orange and purple. As they rode down the main street, townsfolk peered out from windows and doorways, whispering amongst themselves. The Eldon boys pushed through the crowd, leading the party straight to the jailhouse.

Sheriff Anders dismounted with a pained groan and yanked the jailhouse door open. "Get him inside," he barked.

Casey and Tom hauled Slade off the horse, dragging him inside with little regard for his comfort. Slade stumbled, muttering curses under his breath as they tossed him onto the cot in the cell. The iron bars slammed shut behind him, and Anders turned the key in the lock with a satisfying *click*.

"Hope you're more comfortable this time around," Nash muttered as he leaned in the doorway, watching Slade's tired smirk resurface despite the blood on his face.

"Just like old times," Slade wheezed, settling back against the wall.

Before Nash could say anything else, he caught movement outside. Doc Taylor, trudging down the street with his worn medical bag in hand, his face set in a permanent scowl of disapproval. Nash groaned inwardly.

"Looks like you're up next," Willa said, stepping beside him, arms crossed.

"Hell," Nash muttered, turning away from the jailhouse before the doctor could rope him into another round of poking and prodding. "I need a bed, not a damn doctor."

Willa smirked. "You're limping more than usual, cowboy."

"I'm fine," Nash grunted, shoving the whiskey bottle into her hands. "Hold that for me, will ya?"

He made his way down the street toward the saloon, boots dragging against the dirt. The sounds of the town felt distant, muted. He was dead on his feet. All he wanted was the creak of a mattress beneath him and maybe—if the gods were kind—a night without nightmares.

Inside the saloon, the air was thick with cigar smoke and the clink of glasses. The bartender glanced up as Nash walked in, eyeing him warily.

"Howdy, Cowboy," the man grunted, wiping a glass with a rag.

Nash ignored him and dropped a few coins on the counter. "Room."

The bartender took the money, nodding toward the stairs. "Last door on the left."

Nash nodded his thanks and trudged up the stairs, every step making his ribs scream in protest. The corridor was quiet, a blessing he hadn't expected. He reached the door, pushed it open, and stepped inside.

The room was simple—bed, washbasin, a rickety chair by the window—but to Nash, it looked like heaven. He sat down on the edge of the bed, pulling off his boots with a wince. His body felt like it had been through a war, and in a way, it had. He leaned back, closing his eyes just for a moment, the whiskey still warming his belly. He barely noticed when the door creaked open, and Willa's silhouette appeared against the dim light.

"You gonna survive, cowboy?" she asked softly, her voice losing its usual edge.

Nash cracked an eye open and smirked tiredly. "If I wake up, I guess I will."

She tossed the whiskey bottle onto the small table, her lips quirking in something close to a smile. "Get some rest. You earned it."

Nash didn't answer. Sleep was already pulling him under, and for once, he didn't fight it.

The late morning sun streamed weakly through the dusty window, its warmth doing little to ease the stiffness in Nash's bruised ribs. He stirred only when the creak of the door reached his ears. His hand instinctively reached for his Colt, but the scent of coffee and the sight of Willa standing in the doorway stayed his reflex. She was holding a steaming tin cup in one hand and a plate piled with biscuits and eggs in the other.

"You planning on sleepin' all day?" she asked, her tone casual but with a hint of concern beneath it.

Nash groaned and rubbed a hand over his face, his body protesting as he tried to shift. "Might be," he muttered, voice thick with sleep.

Willa set the plate and cup down on the small table by the window. "Figured you'd want somethin' hot in you that ain't whiskey," she said, giving the bottle on the nightstand a pointed glance. "Eat up."

Nash grunted, not bothering to reply, and watched as she left the room, the door shutting behind her with a soft click. He stared at the food for a long moment before dragging himself upright with a wince. The coffee smelled strong, and he reached for it first, taking a careful sip. It scalded his throat, but the bitterness did something to jolt him awake.

He picked at the food, managing a few bites before the effort became too much. His ribs ached with every movement, the dull throb behind his eyes warning him that rest was something his body still needed. He pushed the plate aside and leaned back with a sigh.

His gaze landed on the half-empty whiskey bottle from the night before. Reaching for it, he took several long swigs, feeling the burn slide down his throat and settle in his gut. It wasn't much, but it took the edge off the pain, numbing him enough to think about getting on with the day. The warmth spread slowly, and after a while, Nash sat up, stretching his shoulders carefully. The whiskey was doing its job. He swung his legs over the side of the bed carefully, every movement hurt, and pulled on his boots, grimacing. His body felt like it had been trampled by a herd of cattle, but he wasn't about to lay in bed and wallow.

Standing took effort, but he managed it, bracing himself against the edge of the washstand until the dizziness passed. He glanced in the small, cracked mirror hanging above it—his face looked like hell, bruises dark under his eyes, his stubble thick and untamed. He splashed water on his face, ran a hand through his hair, and stepped toward the door.

Descending the stairs slowly, Nash's boots thudded against the worn wood, the noise loud in the otherwise quiet saloon. A few patrons were scattered around, some nursing drinks despite the early hour, others playing cards in the corner. The bartender glanced up as Nash reached the bottom, giving him a long look before jerking his chin toward the bar.

Willa was there, leaning against the counter, arms crossed over her chest. She looked him over, her gaze settling on the whiskey bottle still clutched in his hand.

"Real healthy breakfast you got there," she said dryly.

Nash smirked, taking another swig before setting the bottle down on the counter with a dull thunk. "Never said I was a sensible man."

Willa shook her head but didn't argue. "Anders'll be wantin' to talk to you soon. Better get yourself together."

Nash sighed, rolling his shoulders. "Soon as I can walk without feelin' like my ribs are about to cave in, I'll be there."

She nodded, pushing a fresh cup of coffee his way. "Then drink this and quit feelin' sorry for yourself."

Nash took the cup with a grunt, feeling the weight of the morning settling heavily on his shoulders. One thing was certain—this day was far from over.

Nash nursed the coffee Willa had shoved into his hands, letting the warmth settle the lingering ache in his ribs. He eyed her over the rim of the cup. "How's Anders?"

Willa leaned against the bar, her arms crossed, a half-smile tugging at her lips. "Doc Taylor patched him up. Bullet went clean through the side of his arm—nothing too serious." She gave him a sideways glance. "He's holed up at the jailhouse, looking real pleased with himself. I already stopped by to see him."

Nash smirked, setting the cup down with a dull thud. "Lookin' to collect your bounty?"

Willa's grin widened. "Damn right. Told you before, Nash—I ain't in this for charity."

Nash arched a brow. "And? Did you get it?"

Her expression soured slightly, but the amusement lingered in her eyes. "Not yet. Sheriff says Slade's gotta swing first. They already lost him once, and he ain't ready to hand over the money just in case."

Nash chuckled, then winced as the motion pulled at his ribs. "Hell," he muttered under his breath, gingerly pressing a hand against his side.

Willa tilted her head at him. "You need to see Anders," she said, her tone shifting to something more serious. "The Eldons are there too, and this whole thing needs clearing up now before someone else gets the wrong idea about you."

Nash sighed, rubbing a hand over his stubbled jaw. "Yeah, reckon you're right. Last thing I need is another fist to the ribs."

Willa pushed off the bar, grabbing her hat from the stool beside her and settling it on her head. "Come on then," she said, heading toward the saloon doors. "Let's get this done before you keel over."

Nash downed the last of the coffee in a single motion, and followed her, his steps slow and measured, every movement sending fresh reminders of the beating he'd taken, each step jarring his ribs. As they stepped outside, the midday sun bore down hard, making the dusty streets shimmer in the heat. The town was alive with murmurs and sideways glances as Nash and Willa made their way down the boardwalk toward the jailhouse.

"They still look at me like I should be swingin' from a tree," Nash muttered, noticing a few hard stares from passing townsfolk.

Willa shrugged. "Guilty or not, they need someone to blame." She cast him a sidelong glance. "Let's make sure it ain't you."

Nash grunted in agreement, adjusting his hat against the glare. "Lead the way."

CHAPTER FIFTEEN

Nash stood just outside the sheriff's office, taking a long, steady breath. The last time he'd walked through that door, it was in shackles, with half the town calling for his neck. Now, things were different—but not by much. He pushed the door open slowly, stepping inside with the cautious air of a man who knew too well how quickly a place could turn hostile.

The familiar scent of gun oil and stale coffee hit him first, mixed with the lingering sting of whiskey and sweat. The room was dimly lit, the afternoon sun filtering through the dust-coated windows in hazy shafts of gold. Sheriff Anders sat behind his desk, his injured arm cradled in a fresh white sling—Doc Taylor's work, no doubt. Despite the wound, Anders looked composed, his good hand resting near the revolver at his hip.

Across from the sheriff, Casey, and Tom Eldon stood stiff and silent. Their eyes cut toward Nash the moment he entered, and for a long beat, the tension in the room tightened like a noose. Nash took in their expressions—hard, weathered, but not as hostile as they'd been before. Maybe Anders had talked some sense into them after all.

Anders leaned back slightly in his chair, tipping his hat up with a weary smirk. "Told the Eldons everything," he said, his voice carrying a note of finality. "Slade and his boys were the ones who gunned down their pa. You helped bring him in."

Nash didn't respond right away. He let the words hang in the air, watching the two brothers carefully. The last time they stood this close, Casey's fists had been pounding into his ribs, and Tom's boot had nearly crushed his throat.

Casey cleared his throat, shifting his weight from one foot to the other, his gaze locking with Nash's. His jaw twitched, and for a moment, Nash thought the man might spit out something harsh, but instead, Casey spoke, his voice rough but measured. "We were wrong." The words came slowly, like they cost him something to say. "Ain't easy for a man to admit, but... you helped take down the bastard that killed our father."

Tom, quieter, nodded stiffly beside him, his lips pressed into a thin line. The younger Eldon didn't say much, but there was something in his eyes—acknowledgment, maybe even the barest hint of respect.

Nash gave them both a slow, steady nod, keeping his face neutral. "Reckon it's water under the bridge," he said, his voice calm but firm. "Long as you know the truth now."

The sheriff snorted. "Truth's a slippery thing in this town. You're lucky it's still worth something to some of us." He gestured toward the cell in the back, where Slade sat slumped on the cot, shackled and silent. Nash glanced over, his brow furrowing when he saw Slade sitting on the cot, his hands resting on his knees. Something was off—too much quiet for a man who never seemed to shut up. Then Nash noticed it: a strip of cloth stuffed into Slade's mouth, tied tight around the back of his head.

Nash smirked. "Looks like you finally found a way to shut him up."

Anders grinned, tapping his fingers on the desk. "Yeah, figured we'd had enough of his mouth. He'll get his say when Judge Guttridge rolls into town. Should be here in a day or so." He leaned forward, looking at Slade with satisfaction. "Until then, he can enjoy the peace and quiet." Slade's eyes burned with fury but bound and gagged; all he could do was glare.

Nash chuckled, wincing at the pull in his side. "Best idea I've heard all week."

Anders nodded toward his deputy, standing near the door. "Your pack's still in the office," he said. "Goin' somewhere?"

Nash stood, adjusting his hat with a slow, deliberate motion. "Think it's best I move on before someone else decides I need killin'," he said, offering a wry smile. "Ironwood's had enough excitement."

Anders gave a short nod, understanding. "Fair enough." He gestured to the deputy. "Fetch his things."

The deputy disappeared into the back room and returned a moment later with Nash's saddlebags, setting them on the desk with a thud. Nash took them, slinging the strap over his shoulder with a quiet grunt of pain. He turned toward the door, pausing just long enough to meet Anders' eyes. "Sheriff," he said with a nod.

Anders returned it. "Nash."

Tom Eldon shifted on his feet, clearing his throat. "If you ever find yourself near the ranch, stop by. Ain't much, but it's honest work."

Nash let out a dry chuckle. "Appreciate it, but I'm not much for settlin' down."

With that, he pushed open the door and stepped out into the sunlight, the heat pressing against him like an old, unwelcome friend. The town still watched him with wary eyes, but Nash didn't pay them any mind. He walked toward the livery, eager to put Ironwood and its troubles behind him.

As he reached the hitching post, Willa leaned against it, arms crossed, watching him with that same unreadable expression she always wore. "So that's it?" she asked. "Just ridin' out?"

Nash nodded. "Figure it's about time."

Willa stepped closer, her boots scuffing the dirt. "You sure you don't want to stick around a while? At least until those ribs of yours are healed."

Nash smirked faintly, shaking his head. "A man like me don't stay in one place for long. You know that."

She raised an eyebrow. "Could be you're runnin' from somethin'. Or someone."

He looked at her then, his gaze steady and searching. "Could be," he said quietly.

For a moment, they stood there in silence, the weight of unsaid things hanging between them. Nash cleared his throat and turned toward his horse, gripping the saddle horn as if it might steady him against the pull he felt toward her.

"You'll be alright," he said, his voice gruff. "You're tough as they come."

Willa chuckled, but there was no humor in it. "Yeah, well, tough don't mean much when you're standin' alone."

Nash froze, her words hitting him harder than he cared to admit. He knew she was right—knew it in the ache that had settled in his chest since the moment he realized he'd have to leave her behind.

The decision was made before he even realized it. Nash's boots scuffed against the dust as he turned back to her, closing the distance between them in two long strides. Willa's eyes flickered with something—defiance, uncertainty—but before she could find the words to push him away, his hand was already at her waist, pulling her close.

"Don't say no," he murmured, his voice low, rough, filled with something he couldn't quite name.

For a fleeting second, Willa stood frozen, her hands braced against his chest. He felt the tension in her, the fight she was weighing in her mind. But then, as if something inside her relented, she leaned in, her fingers curling into the fabric of his shirt. The kiss was tentative at first—hesitant, testing—but it didn't stay that way for long.

She tasted like whiskey and dust and something wilder, something untamed. Nash's grip on her tightened, his thumb grazing the small of her back. The world outside—the creak of a distant wagon, the muffled voices from the saloon—faded into nothing. All that mattered was this moment, the heat between them, the way she responded with a fierce hunger that matched his own.

When they finally pulled apart, Willa's breath came quick, and her cheeks flushed. Her gaze locked on his, and for a moment, something vulnerable passed between them. Then, in true Willa fashion, she ruined it.

"Damn you, Nash," she muttered, though there was no venom in it.

He smirked, brushing a strand of hair back from her face, letting his fingers linger just a little longer than necessary. "I'll take that as a compliment."

Later, under the cover of darkness, they found themselves in Willa's small rented room above the saloon. The space was sparse—just a narrow bed, a rickety table with a half-burned candle, and a single window that rattled in the night breeze. But it felt private like the rest of the world couldn't touch them here.

They moved slowly, each moment stretched thin and deliberate. Willa's touch was unpracticed but sure, her calloused hands tracing the rough lines of scars crisscrossing Nash's chest as if reading the story of his life without a single word spoken. He let her, the weight of her fingers grounding him in a way he hadn't felt in years. His own hands moved with reverence, exploring the shape of her back, the curve of her hips, as if committing her to memory.

The lantern cast long, flickering shadows across the walls, and the floorboards creaked beneath their shifting weight. They came together with an intensity that was more than just desire—there was something else beneath it, something deeper and more dangerous.

Nash wasn't a man who put down roots, and Willa wasn't a woman who waited for anyone. They both knew this couldn't last. But for now, in the hush of the night, it was enough.

When it was over, Nash lay staring at the ceiling, feeling Willa's steady breathing against his chest. His fingers idly traced patterns along her arm, his thoughts drifting. He didn't want to think about what came next—riding out of Ironwood, leaving her behind. But the trail always called, and Nash never stayed in one place for long.

Willa stirred, propping herself up on one elbow, looking down at him with that same mix of fire and softness that had drawn him in from the start. "You leavin' tomorrow?" she asked, her voice quiet, but he could hear the weight behind it.

Nash exhaled slowly, his hand trailing from her arm to her waist. "Reckon so," he said.

She didn't argue. She just nodded, lying back down and resting her head against him.

Neither of them said another word. There wasn't any need.

The next morning, Nash rose early, the sunlight flooding through the window, casting a golden glow over the room. Willa stirred beside him, her hair tousled and her breathing even. He took a moment to watch her, committing the sight to memory.

When she finally opened her eyes, she found him sitting on the edge of the bed, lacing his boots.

"Already?" she asked, her voice husky with sleep.

Nash nodded, glancing over his shoulder. "You know how it is."

Willa sat up, pulling the blanket around her shoulders. "You ever think about settlin' down? Findin' somethin'... steadier?"

He turned to her, his expression softening. "I think about a lot of things. But the trail's all I know."

Willa looked at him for a long moment, then smiled faintly. "Guess I'll just have to wait and see if it ever leads you back this way."

Nash stood, picking up his hat and placing it on his head. "I reckon it might. Someday."

She nodded, her smile turning wry. "Don't make me come huntin' you down, cowboy."

He chuckled, leaning down to press a lingering kiss to her forehead. "I wouldn't dream of it."

As Nash rode out of Ironwood, the town fading into the distance behind him, he felt a strange mix of emotions. His name was cleared, justice had been served, and the road stretched wide open before him. But for the first time in a long while, he felt the faint pull of something other than the trail—a place, a person, a possibility.

The horizon beckoned, as it always did. But this time, Nash rode with the hope that someday, the trail might circle back. And when it did, he knew exactly where he'd want it to lead.

The End

Please don't close the book just yet!

I'd like to thank you for reading, your time has been much appreciated, and I am heartened that you reached the end. This has been a work of love to bring back to life the tales left so many years ago by my grandfather's father in his journals.

Stories of the old west, of times long forgotten and from people telling them as recent events. It has been a humbling experience to record these events and bring them back to life nearly 150 years later.

If you could spare a few moments to leave this ol' writer a review, and in doing so you'll be leaving one for the writer of the original journals, Declan Kelly, and those whose lives you've read about.

Next Book in the series – Echoes of the Gunfighter

Printed in Dunstable, United Kingdom

71542108R00107